D1384921

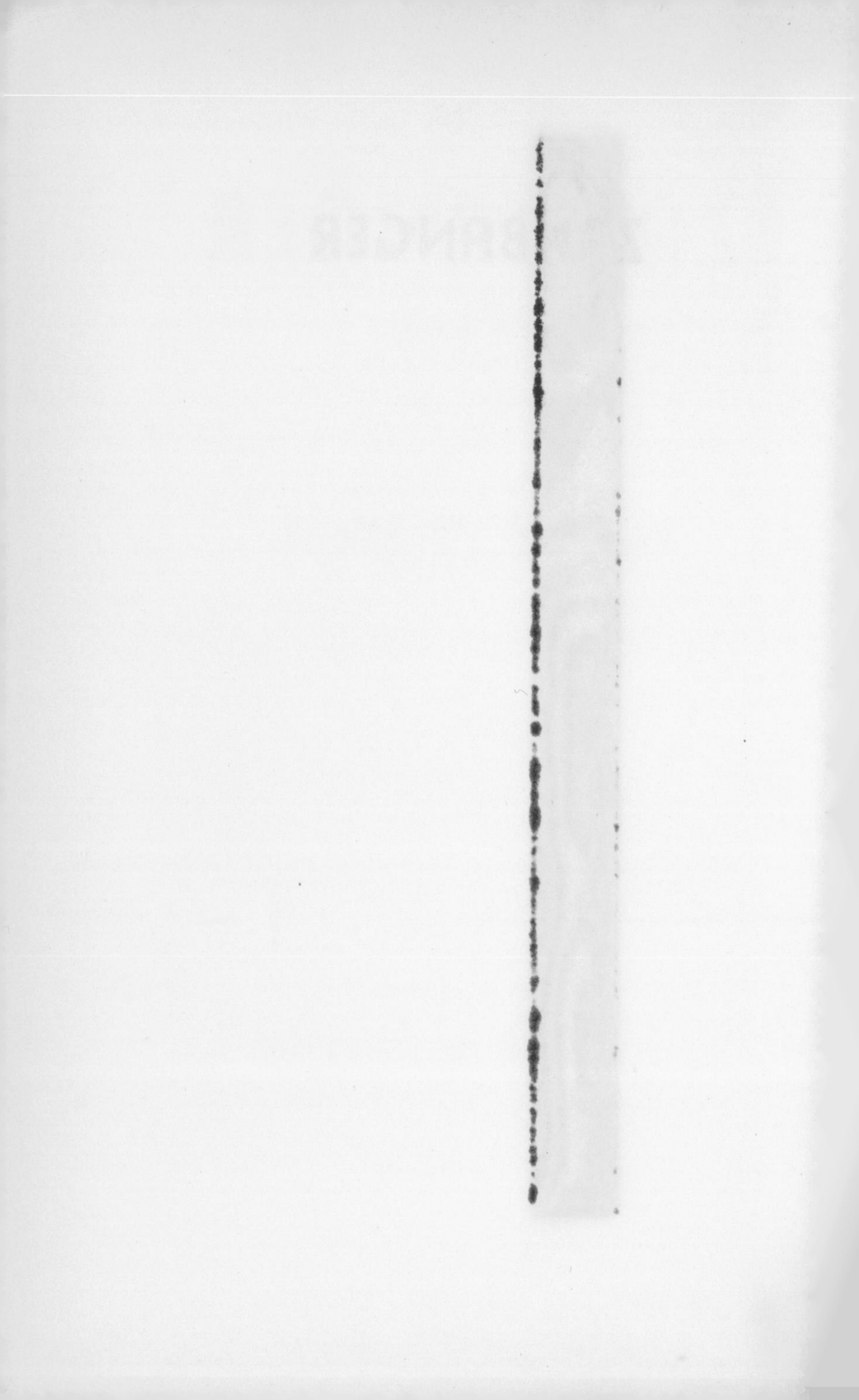

ZANBANGER

By R. R. Knudson

ZANBALLER
SPORTS POEMS (editor, with P. K. Ebert)
JESUS SONG
YOU ARE THE RAIN
FOX RUNNING

ZANBANGER

by R. R. Knudson

HARPER & ROW, PUBLISHERS
New York, Hagerstown, San Francisco, London

Printed in the United States of America. For information address Harper & Row, Publishers, Inc., 10 East 53rd Street, New York, N.Y. 10022. Published simultaneously in Canada by Fitzhenry & Whiteside Limited, Toronto.
First Edition

Library of Congress Cataloging in Publication Data
Knudson, R Rozanne, 1932–
Zanbanger.

SUMMARY: A teenage girl encounters problems when she tries to play on the boys' high school basketball team.
[1. Sex role—Fiction 2. Basketball—Fiction]
I. Title.
PZ7.K785Zap3 [Fic] 75-25416
ISBN 0-06-023213-7
ISBN 0-06-023214-5 lib. bdg.

For Alexander, Christopher, Conrad, Danny,
Garth, Hal, Jamie, Jay, Karl, Kent, Lee,
Rod, Ryan, Steele, Timmy, Zane—my nephews.
And for Christie, my niece.
Fellow ballplayers, all.

ZANBANGER

Chapter 1

TAPTAPTAPTAPTAP!

TAP! TAp! Tap! tap.

Thuds. Thud.

Carpenters laid down their hammers, wiped their brows, and stood up to admire the glittering floor they'd just finished. Their foreman doffed his hard hat at the crowd. He announced, "This Robert E. Lee Junior-Senior High School gymnasium is ready for business."

Basketball business, he meant. Finally, finally our season could begin. I grinned at my pal Rinehart. I thumped him right on top of his genius head. I felt the new boards under my feet. They weren't warped anymore. They weren't all rotten and pitted like they used to be. Now our dribbles wouldn't bounce into the bleachers by accident. Now our set shots wouldn't be lopsided. We'd soon be practicing our free throws and lay-ups and rebounds. After that we'd be playing games. Then winning our league. Then on to the *Herald* Tournament—

Ta-pa-da. Ouch.

Ta-ouch. Oh, ouch!

Another hammer, but this one so feeble I could hardly hear it over the kids shuffling their feet and snickering. I looked at the big shots squatting down in center court. Our principal, F. Parnell Manfred, seemed to be banging his dumb thumb.

"Gentlemen and ladies. Boys and girls. I personally will drive a nail in tribute to this grand beginning for our glorious team," he said into the microphone.

Tapsi.

"Oh, and a lucky nail for all you wonderful, wonderful reporters gathered here from our Arlington County, Virginia, newspapers."

Flashbulbs popped but it was taps for that nail, too. It went in sideways at the center-jump circle. I whispered to Rinehart, "I'll remember those stubs when I whiz downcourt. Don't want to puncture the basketball."

Rinehart didn't bother to whisper. "I can't have you injured, Zan. I'll claw them out soon as this gushy ceremony's over." He opened his pocketknife, same one he used to dissect toads in his basement laboratory. Impatiently he examined the blade.

Tap. Thunk. "There now, dear parents, teachers, and boosters of the Generals basketball team." Our principal brushed sawdust from his brown office shoes and straightened one red sock. He poked his tie back inside the shiniest black suit in Virginia. He wasn't known as a swell dresser. He was mostly known as a meatball.

"Check his feet," I couldn't help mumbling. "He'll ruin our championship floor with his scuffy heels."

"He means well," Rinehart said, his absolute worst criticism of someone.

Manfred continued. "We are gathered here this Monday, this second day of January, to cut a blue ribbon and throw out the first basketball. Come forward, come forward, Randy Boyle of our very own Generals."

Suddenly the gym filled up with screams. Just the sight of Randy in his letter sweater sent kids into

He's our guy
He's our dream
Randy's captain
Of our team.
Yea!

Lurleen Dewey led that cheer. Ruby Jean Twilly twirled her baton and strutted alongside Randy, who grabbed the scissors from Mr. Manfred and slashed the mid-court ribbon with a flourish. He bowed low. He pranced in place while Manfred bumbled around looking for a ceremonial basketball. He found one on the far foul line. He wobbled a pass to Randy.

Randy knew what to do next. He dribbled behind his back the full length of the court, changing hands, weaving in and out of imaginary opponents. He flipped the ball between his legs, backpedaled, and caught it. He lunged toward the basket, leapt, and while still airborne, turned 360 degrees. He slam-dunked a shot that could be heard cross-county.

Everyone in the gym but me and Rinehart held up two fingers for Randy's two points. Rinehart said, "He's an egomaniac." I didn't say anything because I was too busy wishing I could dunk baskets. For that you have to be tall. Not really as tall as Randy, but taller than me, for sure. I watched Randy leap again and cling by one hand to the rim. He called for a teammate.

Out of the crowd streaked Fritz Slappy, another General. He tossed Randy the red-white-and-blue ball—new this year in the boys' league. A real pro ball. Randy dropped from the rim but kept hold of his treasure, shouting, "Turn on the scoreboard, Freak. I'll show these folks some points!"

Freak?

He meant me. Or Arthur Rinehart, my "alter ego," as Rinehart himself would say. Randy hated us both. Me because I hung around the gym a lot—this one and the YMCA over in Clarendon. I wanted to work out. I wanted to practice my set shots in between times when the boys got "their" gym—which was most of the time. And I never rooted for Randy like the other girls. Lurleen Dewey had reported to him what I said at a football game last fall. "I can't encourage that show-off creep with a cheer. Here—take this dumb pom-pom," I'd told her.

He's still a creep. And I'm his freak. Also Rinehart. Randy hates him for being my unathletic pal. Once in gym class he belted Rinehart for dropping a pop fly. "You got hands like sieves, fellow. You couldn't catch a watermelon. Why don'tcha take off those thick glasses so you can play some outfield?"

"Secret strategy," Rinehart told Randy then. He never lets anyone outtalk or outthink him. Arthur Rinehart: smartest schemer at Robert E. Lee. Winner of two out of three science fairs he's entered. Always A+ in everything. As uncoordinated as Silly Putty, but my best friend for five years in a row. We know each other's moves. He fumbles baseballs and footballs and basketballs. I catch and throw them; and he's my private coach.

Hardly anyone paid attention to Mr. Manfred now that Randy had seized the spotlight. Our principal shouted his speech into a hand microphone. "And in conclusion—conclusion—an extra added treat for our glamorous lady Generals—"

I couldn't believe my ears. Manfred mentioned—

"Our Generalettes!" he hollered.

My team! I was sure he'd never remember those mighty basketballers. Polly and Joan and E.J. and Millie and Phyllis and all of us, ready to trounce the Admiralettes and Judgettes and Wolfettes on our way to the girls' *Herald* Tournament. Last year they all thrashed us good. But then last year I hadn't perfected my spot shooting, and E.J. wasn't as tall as she'd grown over the summer, and Millie—

Mr. Manfred broke into my dream of the *Herald* trophy. He bellowed, "I've ordered the Generalettes' locker room completely redecorated. For that special flair in interior styling, we have our girls' PE teacher and basketball coach to thank. I give you Mrs. Evelyn Butor."

No one wanted to see her. We all knew she weighed two hundred pounds in the shade. Kids came streaming out of the stands, running for school buses and cars. Manfred mingled with the big shots, shaking hands, posing for pictures. I heard him bragging to Ronald Mergler, Jr., *Herald* reporter, that the Generals had it made, what with players like Randy Boyle, Fritz Slappy, "Fighting" Eugene Matello, and Ben Brown, tallest center in the league. "And there's our fantastically successful Coach O'Hara!" Manfred practically swooned about "his" team.

Plus don't forget our girls' team! I wanted to bellow, too. I wanted Mr. Mergler to sharpen his pencil and write our story. I almost snuck over to where he stood taking notes about Coach O'Hara, but Rinehart wouldn't let me mess around with publicity. "You'll show him this season. No need to *woo* him. Come with me, Zan. Let's tour the girls' locker room while everyone's watching Boyle and Manfred. It's my only chance to see if Mrs. Butor got rid of those mildewy shower curtains you always complain about."

"Rinehart, I'm with you," I answered as usual.

We crept backwards through the swinging door. We listened. Dark in there and silent. Not even the water pipes leaking. At first I could make out only shadowy lockers, benches, and our same chlorine footbath. I could smell it all the way from our shower room. I bumped into a tall, cold object and held on, feeling around for the light switch. There. In the dim light of a bare bulb overhead, I discovered I'd been playing footsie with a new scale, the standing-up kind like in a doctor's office. Rinehart hopped aboard. He fiddled with the weights until he seemed satisfied that the needle stayed put. "Three pounds over my laboratory scale," he pronounced. "Inaccurate, as I might have guessed."

"Who needs it?" I said, looking here and there for other new equipment. Like a whirlpool bath for aching muscles. Like a rubdown table and a cabinet full of tape and iodine and knee guards and wrist sweatbands. The boys' locker room has that stuff. More, even. A steam bath. A sauna bath. I happened to know.

"Girls get injured, too, Rinehart. We could use around a half-pint of the old Mercurochrome. Instead we get dumb scales." I slid the weights to zero.

Rinehart stepped on and off the scales, trying to adjust them. "These will be helpful. Instruments of science always are. Basketball's a running game. The less fatty tissue, the faster you and your team will run. The less tired you'll get. Tired players commit errors. You'll want to check weights every day, before and after practice."

"Oh, never mind that, Rinehart. Where's our wall-to-wall carpet, our trophy cases, our autographed citations from the school board, our banners and pennants all over the place like next door in the boys' palace? Randy even has his name and a gold star painted on his locker." I pointed to our lockers, now that we could seem them. "Lookit. They're still dangling half off their hinges. But—ech! Painted maroon. My worst color. And these matching icky curtains block out the sun. How can I see whether I've caught a dose of athlete's foot from this floor? Ech! Maroon linoleum. Couldn't Mrs. Butor remember that's Swanson's team color, not ours?"

Rinehart didn't seem to be listening. He consulted a chart tacked on the wall. "These body weights are for beauty, not for athletics," he said under his breath. "They don't account for girls' muscle structure. Hmmmmm."

Near the weight chart I noticed an uncracked mirror. Now *that* must be new. Aileen will love it. She always insists the other one gives her old-age lines. She'll also love the full-length mirror on the far wall and the tinted mirror next to that. "I can't believe it," I hollered. "All these mirrors. For looks? You call these helpers, when what we need is a big blackboard for diagramming plays? And locks on these."

I kicked my old locker. "My ruler gets stolen around twice a week from this."

Rinehart kept his eyes fastened to the weight chart and scribbled numbers on a clipboard he always carried.

"The same goes for these dopey mottoes." I stormed over to the nearest Magic Marker sign. I read PRETTY IS AS PRETTY DOES. "Who printed this?"

Rinehart said, "Most probably the interior decorator herself—Evelyn Butor." He sat me down on a bench. "Zan, don't kick lockers. You might injure your toes, and toes play an important part in balance. Basketball's a game of balance." He disappeared into the shower room. I heard water, like every tap was running at once. "I'm testing the temperature," he called. "I want to find out if it's hot enough to kill bacteria."

Steam poured from the showers, so I couldn't see another framed motto. Anyway I'd already recognized the handwriting. Mrs. Butor's, for sure. I remembered the curlicue F's she'd put on my report cards so far this semester. For volleyball, F because I played "too aggressively." For folk dancing, F because I cut up in class. F in modern dancing because I cut class every day. At that rate I'd F the whole year in gym class. "I'm flunking my favorite subject," I called.

But didn't have to. Rinehart stood beside me, barefoot. "I almost broke my leg stepping out of your slimy footbath," he complained. He shook a corked test tube. "I've taken a sample of the muck. I'll run it through my lab tonight." With that he sat down on an old splintery bench. I held his clipboard while he wiggled into his socks.

"Rinehart, could you hear me in there?" I was hoping for his wise advice. He's older than me. He'll know what to do. "I'm failing PE—"

"You're no such thing. You're the best athlete in Robert E. Lee Junior-Senior High. Why do you think I go around with you? Opposites attract, as Mrs. Butor might scrawl on your locker-room walls." He waved vaguely to a nearby motto. He wiped steam from his glasses and buckled his floppy galoshes. "Besides, I'm studying your sports career for science. Your strength, agility, stamina, quickness, accuracy. Your mental attitude. Your speed in learning new techniques and—and schemes. My next science-fair project will prove once and for all that girls are as—"

E.J. just then swung through the hall door and said, "A search party's on its way here. Four of them. Mrs. Butor's touring with certain of her favorites." E.J. struck a basketball pose in front of the full-length mirror. Her eyes got serious. "Hook shots from the circle. I'm surrounded by defenders. I'm up—up—"

I caught the spirit. "E.J. glides toward her guard. She swoops, floats, dazzles, hooks—"

"None of those," Rinehart said. "For that shot you bring the ball directly over your head. You shoot and follow through by swinging your whole body toward the basket." He didn't look up from the locker hinge he was screwing together with his toad knife. He rattled off directions for the perfect hook. Rinehart couldn't zap the ball through the hoop himself from anywhere on court, but he sure could memorize the coaching books he read. He glanced up at E.J. "That pose is more like it. Okay, Zan. Ask Butor to assign you this locker I've repaired. Here on the end, for better circulation. Your uniform will dry properly."

We heard Mrs. Butor's voice down the hall but coming nearer. "Gals, you'll simply love your dressing room. It's divine. Vanity mirrors! Ruffled curtains stitched in our own home ec department. Your lockers alive with glowing color—"

"Swanson's Admiralettes' color," E.J. said, just then noticing maroon.

"A wonderful scale to help us keep slim for our menfolks." I heard Mrs. Butor's clunky footsteps at the door. I heard *Ooooooo*'s and *Ahhhhhhhhh*'s from Ruby Jean Twilly, Lurleen Dewey, and Dee-Dee Tupper as they shimmied into Maroon City.

We three basketballers bolted for the gym, where we'd be safe from Mrs. Butor. I said, "Those majorettes and cheerleaders never suit up for PE class. Why do they need to use our locker room?"

"To polish the sequins on their halters," E.J. whispered across the now empty court.

"To strut in front of mirrors." I answered my own question. I began to strut in a zigzag pattern. Little slow steps, then faster as I grew used to the unwarped floor. I ran. Faster and faster, basket to basket. I pretended to dribble. I put moves on imaginary players. I broke free for a shot, hauled down my phantom rebound with a full sweeping motion of my arms. I stood on my favorite spot and practiced some fakes. Hand fakes: I threw my hands up with the ball but kept my feet on the shiny floor. My imaginary guard went up; I slipped away. Head fakes: I twisted my head upward so my guard would think I planned to jump. I didn't. I passed to E.J., who pretended I'd stung her hands with the ball.

"Great fun," she said and laughed.

"Rinehart, come and coach us," I urged my pal. He rose from the center circle, where he'd clawed up those two bent nails. He stuck them carefully under the clip of his board. He rolled us a ball from under the bleachers. He turned on the scoreboard at the switch box. "Who wants to be home team?"

"I'll be the visitor," I said, chasing E.J. one on one.

We played in earnest now, with Rinehart calling instructions. E.J. dribbled, faked me out, and shot. Swish. I drove the sidelines and shot. Swish. She arched one in from twenty-five feet. Swish. I screeched down the middle and popped a jumper—my nearest shot to the dunk. Kerplunk. The gym lost its smell of lumber and turpentine. I tasted my wet hair instead. Salt stung my eyes. E.J.'s forehead gleamed. As we tired, our moves against each other grew ragged.

"Work together now. Together," Rinehart advised us. We dribbled and shot, rebounded, shot, dribbled some more. "A pass travels four times faster than a dribble," Rinehart corrected us. "Speed up your game."

Chest passes, bounce passes, overhand, underhand, we shucked off imaginary defenders and rifled or lobbed to each other in spurts.

"Run. Run. Run."

I could barely breathe after a while. My sweaty blue jeans stuck to my knees with each step. E.J.'s T-shirt looked like a puddle. We flopped in the bleachers, exhausted. I folded my dead arms. E.J. tied back her hair to show us both her drenched nape.

"This is nothing, Zan. Zero compared to how hard you'll be slaving to catch up on other teams. Remember—your whole league's been practicing for weeks while you've waited for this." He tapped the new floor with his clipboard. He rolled me the ball again, a perfect grounder. "Starting tomorrow at your first official workout—"

"Starting this minute," I answered. With heavy legs I moved toward the basket, E.J. trudging after. The scoreboard lit our game so far.

HOME 34 VISITORS 34

I limped to my favorite spot for a shot. I sent off the ball with numb fingertips. Swish. E.J. had enough strength for one pat on my back. "You do that as well as Randy."

"Both of you do," called Rinehart. "Now faster tempo. Don't loiter. Run. Rush. Pass. Keep eyes on target, shoot, rebound, control, control scientifically, come up court with E.J., Zan . . ."

Chapter 2

Tuesday's basketball practice. At last! After an hour of punctuating sentences in English class. After my dumb general science course. After chorus, a history quiz, an endless study hall. After a lunch of bread, bread, bread—an entire loaf Rinehart forced me to eat with no bologna on it, no cheese or honey. Before practice I'm supposed to feast on carbohydrates. Nothing else. Rinehart's scientific plan for me. Boring, but I could already feel tons of stamina zipping through my bloodstream while I changed into my sweat suit. Finally to practice. Hide my ruler. Slam my locker. Out the maroon door to a gym full of teammates. Snatch a brown ball and shoot.

Ah.

"Put the ball through this iron hoop. That's the whole point of playing," I shouted to anyone standing around. I tossed a swisher from just over the center line. From way back there, I was hoping to get deadly. Sink 'em every time when no one comes out that far to guard me. I kept shooting. Two out of two, three out of five, five out of nine. "Joan—Phyllis—Millie—everyone, get with it. Play up. Aileen, guard me so I can fake some fakes."

Aileen leaned against a bleacher, fiddling with her pink fuzzy socks. "I'll wait till Mrs. Butor arrives. Don't want to soil my outfit unless I have to. These leotards simply wilt in our stuffy gym." She turned a neat sock cuff. Otherwise she didn't budge.

She also wore her tights, left over from dance class. I'd never bought a pair. I hated pink. I hated the pinchy legs. I hated dancing. I'd flunked PE all fall while workmen tore up the gym floor and we girls were banished to the home ec wing. Up there, we'd pushed back stoves and tripped around because Mrs. Butor said there wasn't enough room to play ball. Down here in the gym—plenty of room.

Ah.

Far downcourt, E.J. sank baskets from the free-throw line, her best spot. One after another. Hardly ever touching the shatterproof glass backboard. Swish. Swish. Steady-handed E.J. She called to me, "Mrs. Butor may never arrive. Tonight's her square-dance club, remember. She's probably home resting."

My teammates stood talking in small groups or fooled around on the sidelines. Joan tried to dribble to the top of the bleachers. She lobbed a shot from there. POW, against a rafter. Millie chased JoJo Rice from vaulting horse to trampoline, ready to bop her with a ball she held high with one big hand. Charlotte slung her ball cross-court, where it crashed into a circle of gossipers.

"All the way," I shouted for that ball. "Throw it. Hustle, gang. We've only got forty-five minutes before the Generals overrun this gym." I began to take lay-ups, hoping a line would form behind me. I dribbled fast, jumped—a high jump, not a broad jump. I shot, careful to bank the ball off the backboard. "The closer to the backboard you are, the better chance you have," I called to Bumpy. She rebounded and passed to Teeny, who waited in the growing line.

We drilled and drilled. Like this: Begin with both feet square on the floor. Start toward the basket. Catch the ball from whoever rebounds it. Dribble, raise right knee, bring ball up, keep ball balanced in the palm, release ball, flex fingers in a follow-through, take short steps to the left of the basket, and join the rebounding line. Rinehart had taught me perfectly.

"Crash the boards," I told rebounders. "Drop on in there, brownie," I invited our regulation ball into the net.

Splat. Spin. Not in.

Generalettes were sports-rusty after months of dancing. A December full of ballet had ruined their timing. Their footwork was too delicate, their shooting too dainty. Their punchless lay-ups floated like feathers in Swan Lake. Their puny rebounding could never take us to the *Herald* Tournament. Polly kept stopping mid-shot to dab at her brow with a Kleenex. Aileen quit when a loose ball broke the clasp on her ankle bracelet. After a while Teeny panted, "Time out forever."

I dashed around, trying to incite some spirit. I played guard now with quick, mean moves, hoping to fluster Millie then Putt then JoJo then Charlotte on their way down the shooting lanes. I went left, right, flapped my hands and stomped my feet. My body tried to keep theirs off balance and away from the backboard. But still I shouted encouragement.

"Blow by me. Fake me out. Attack. Attack. Roar and soar. Beau-teee-ful shot."

Splat. Kerplunk off the rim.

"Pour it on. Okay, okay. Don't let me mug you. Phyllis, good position. Slam and jam. Shoot. Shoot."

Swish. But swish in air, way outside the basket. The net never touched the ball.

"Drive. Drive. Play gutsy, Joan. Don't mind if I hang on you. Run and gun. Attaboy."

"Gals, gals, gals," Mrs. Butor called from the hall door. Halfway through it, she was still twice as huge as anyone on our team, even seniors. Very fat, our coach. She lumbered along the out-of-bounds line and settled on the lowest bleacher seat like a grounded blimp. She said "Gals" more times. She gestured for a ball.

I coughed one up. It slapped her palms hard. Aileen crossed the court, ready now to mess up her cuffs and unarrange her barrettes. E.J. jogged from the free-throw line. She rolled her eyes at me; I wet my lips with a stuck-out tongue. Our usual greeting when we used to meet in Mrs. Butor's dance class.

But today we weren't dancing. No, man! This was our first basketball practice of the season, and our coach just lounged there, smiling. Come on, Butor. We have catching-up to do. Let's hit the boards, I thought, watching her delve into her shoulder bag. She pulled out a small brown book, *Official Guide to Girls' Basketball.* I saw the title from where I jumped in place, trying to keep my legs from cooling off. I needed to play ball.

"We're all gals here, not boys," Butor said first off. "For us, basketball is not a rowdy game"—she looked directly at me—"nor is it a contact sport." She sat fast and waited.

Aileen retied her shoelaces into fancy bows. Millie,

suddenly embarrassed by her soaking shirt, cringed into the team. Putt swiped her chin with the tail of Joan's shirt. My own sweat stains, huge as Texas, didn't bother me. "When do we start swishing them in there again?" I asked, pointing to the hoop.

"Again? I observed no one scoring baskets! Your guarding was much too aggressive, Suzanne!"

Suzanne. No one else in the world called me my real name, not even Rinehart in his worst mood. I couldn't think what to say back.

Yes I could. *Moron. Imbecile.* And *cretin.* Words Rinehart used to describe Mrs. Butor. And his favorite Latin—*rufus gigantus dodo.* Translated, it means "giant red-faced dimwit." But if I yelled that, I'd be sent to the leaky showers early. So I only said my nickname: "Zan."

Mrs. Butor ignored me. Lazily she stood up. I noticed her feet for the first time. Not sneakers. Not even street shoes, her usual clonkers with the six-inch platforms. Instead she wore ballet slippers. E.J. squeezed my elbow. "At least they aren't tap-dance shoes," she whispered.

Tapping's finally over, I knew, feeling the solid wood beneath me. Feeling my legs full of carbohydrates and my feet in trusty Keds. Let's go, I thought, even if we scrimmage to Chopin. "The boys get this gym in another fifteen minutes," I muttered loud enough for even a dimwit to hear.

She heard. She led us on court and bent to pat her knees. "Gals, are we ready to work hard? Then limber, limber. Touch your toes and the floor. One, two, three, four." She, of course, could barely reach her thighs. "Gals, follow me in this arm exercise." Butor rose to tiptoes and aimed for the roof. "Shoulders up, hands high, two, three." Her face changed color—from red to maroon. Soon she puffed numbers.

And so did the Generalettes.

What nonsense, three, four. I almost shouted, You're wasting time. We need to run, not jiggle. I grumbled to myself. We need to build up our lungs for those ten grueling games this season. The Generals already sprint two miles a day, I happen to know. Rinehart's been keeping a log of their practice sessions at the YMCA. He sneaks in there and watches.

I slithered close to our coach. I said, "See these brown balls, Mrs. Butor? When do we get to shoot them?" I pointed to a limp net.

"Two *gasp* three *gasp* four *gasp*—"

Some answer!

I decided to sit this one out. I snaked from the exercise line. Still counting, I backed into bleachers near the boys' locker room. I could hear them behind the door, suiting up. They yelled jokes to each other. They flipped towels and ripped tape. I looked down at my own ankles, hidden by floppy socks. I started wishing out loud, in case Mrs. Butor might pay attention. "I wish girls got tape to protect our bones and hold up our socks! I wish we could scrimmage instead of playing slimnastics. Wish we had uniforms instead of—"

"Psssst."

"I wish—"

"Pssssst, Zan. May I cut into your fantasy?" Rinehart's voice came from somewhere under the bleachers. I ducked to discover him perched on a stack of books. From there he could see the messy line of knee benders. He looked sick. He said, "According to my stopwatch, your team has fifty-nine more seconds on this court before Randy leads his troops out that door." He nodded toward the noise. "And according to my log of the Generals"—he turned pages in a thick notebook—"you should be practicing team defense right now to keep up with them."

Fifty-nine seconds! Team defense! I was mad enough to call from the bleachers, "Mrs. Butor. Please could we try some fast breaks? With man-to-man coverage? Or—"

Sparks of sweat flew from her chin. "Suzanne, return to your position in line. You must cooperate with my team as we limber together."

I zinged the nearest ball at her "team." "Warm up? I never cooled off from last season when we didn't win. Please, couldn't we try—"

"Suzanne, if you hope to play for me, you must follow my lead. Join us."

Just then, Randy Boyle burst into the scene, flanked by DumDum Cadden and followed by the rest of his Generals. Every guy was ruddy from a rubdown. Every one wore miles of tape and yards of new silk. Their blue-and-gray uniforms had their names in block letters a mile high: BOYLE, CADDEN, MATELLO, CUNNINGHAM, SLAPPY. No crowd would ever wonder who. They spun tricolored basketballs. They eyed our cotillion. They winked at us and at each other.

Randy aimed a pass at my lap. "Hey, bench sitter," he hollered. "I didn't know the garbage man gave you his uniform." He let fly.

And I dropped the ball.

Chapter 3

Miserable Wednesday. Sleet fell all over me and Rinehart on our hike to school. He slogged along in his galoshes, dodging puddles, careful to keep dry. I turned every pothole full of slush into a fountain. Stomp. Stomp. Ice gushed from my basketball shoes. So what? I'd never need them again. I wasn't about to knee-bend through Butor's routines.

Dumb, gross, icky basketball exercises.

My wet blue jeans clung to my frozen socks. I shook a fist in the direction of school. "Take that, Mrs. Butor." Underwater I felt a shoelace pop. Next the tread would come loose and slap floors all day. So what? I'd be buying some common old exercise shoes for the season.

Ahead of me, Rinehart threaded his way across the snowy football field, his usual shortcut. Every morning my pal made me run from goalpost to goalpost while he kept time on his stopwatch and took notes—tons of notes. About my movements, my "style," Rinehart said. About my improvements. About how I compare in speed and stamina to Randy, Fritz, DumDum, and Eugene. He'd timed them during football workouts. "For my science-fair project concerning your fine Generals," he'd told Coach O'Hara, who believed him and let him attend scrimmages. He remembered Rinehart's first prizes. Coach O'Hara loves a winner.

Ahead, Rinehart called, "No wind sprints today. You'd try so hard you'd pull a tendon in these snowdrifts. But you must run extra laps at practice this afternoon."

"What practice? Oh, you mean limbering? Or whatever Butor's doing to us."

"I mean at a practice that I've planned for you—Plan A!" He waved his briefcase at Lee High. "Let's take your favorite shortcut."

We stole through the gym. Coach O'Hara's light showed under his office door. He's probably snug in there writing mottoes for Randy and Company: Second best is nothing. That sounds like Coach. Winning's not a matter of life or death. It's more important than either. Or perhaps right this minute Coach is stalking his locker room, making sure a batch of clean towels awaits the Generals after their first home game tonight. Towels and oranges and Gatorade. Champagne, maybe. Oh—I wish he were my coach.

"Hey, Rinehart, it's the boys' home opener tonight. And us girls aren't even shooting lay-ups yet. Oh, the pain!"

"What?" He couldn't hear me under his earmuffs. He fell in beside my sopping Keds. His glasses slipped down his nose, useless there and anyway fogged over. But his feet were dry, weren't they? And his slide rule safe in his briefcase with his thermometer. That's all he cares about. Science! He doesn't want to play ball.

"Oh, no one cares," I cried to the rafters. "Cares, cares, cares" echoed in the empty court.

"I care," Rinehart said back, gloomy as me.

I looked at my pal all covered with scarves and gloves and an overcoat practically down to his galoshes. He was trying to fish a book from the plastic bagful he carried. He was trying to unsnap his briefcase and show me more dumb papers. He could hardly stay balanced. He nearly tripped on his own clipboard. "How could you care?" I asked him. "You've never felt the sting of a fast pass. You've never outslicked your guard and slammed past for two points. How does it feel to outthink a defense? How does it feel to swish a basket? How would you know, Arthur Rinehart?"

I helped him gather his junk. I opened a hall door and we plunged into the morning crowd. "I know precisely how you feel," said Rinehart before he left me at my homeroom. "See you in English." He darted away, swift for him.

Kids in homeroom stood singing the Lee fight song.

> Lee High will shine tonight,
> Lee High will shine.
> Lee High will shine tonight,
> All down the line.
> We're all dressed up tonight,
> That's one good sign.
> When the sun goes down
>   and the moon comes up,
> Lee High will shine.

I kept mum. I couldn't waste my lungs pepping the Generals while my own team fell apart. Around four verses later, a couple of tears dripped on my desk.

Nobody noticed my clenched teeth. The flag hung unsaluted. Our teacher didn't call the roll. On basketball-game days, everything sacred got dumped.

Kids cheered in the halls as Generals passed. Fritz Slappy fled a mob of seventh-graders who wanted to touch his sweater. Eugene Matello and Ben Brown signed their names to a girl's broken-arm cast. Down the main steps, Ruby Jean Twilly led a parade of rooters just when I tried to climb up to English.

Rinehart beat me there. From under his coat he produced a towel, a fleecy square embroidered with *Generals.* "Dry off, Zanner. Especially your hair," he told me. He rubbed my ears until I cried "Ouch." Then he handed me clean gym socks from his overcoat pocket and a pair of pretty good shoelaces. "Randy's," he said. "He cares!"

"Like heck he cares. He hates us." I knew Rinehart had raided Randy's locker. He'd probably picked the lock with his toad-dissecting knife. "Did you remember to snitch his uniform for me?" I whispered, because Fuzzy Harrison, our English teacher, was lecturing about commas.

Rinehart didn't laugh at my question. "You could fit it" is what he said. He held out a roll of tape. "Randy's." He gave me a ruler. "Randy's—he cares about your math grade, too." Then he laughed.

I put on Randy's socks, relaced my shoes, taped the soles tight, and had time left over for listening to commas. Rinehart wrote in his log all period, tons of words he didn't show me until on our way to chorus. Then he flipped pages before my eyes and tried to explain his Plan A. "I'll use it as part of my science fair project—all very experimental—observational—

accurate biologically—precise measurements—" He had to shout over Lurleen Dewey's electric megaphone.

> Basketball . . . Basketball . . .
> Basketball . . . Boys
> You play basketball
> We'll make the noise.

We sang loud in chorus to drown out that noise. Then Rinehart took off for advanced-placement biology, and I pushed through a wall of pom-pom girls to my lowly general science course.

I hate science. I hadn't cracked a book all semester, not even to study for the final exam, which was about to happen on the sixteenth of January, same day as our first Generalettes basketball game. I'd be as prepared for that exam as our team would be for Swanson's Admiralettes. Zero prepared. Unless Rinehart saved me again. And saved our team with his Plan A. More likely Scheme A. Rinehart never simply plans.

I slipped a note to E.J. beside me: "Rinehart's going one-on-one against Butor today in practice," I'd scribbled. She gave me a quizzical smile while concentrating on the blackboard. Fine student, E.J. She always beats me in science, A to D. Also in commas. Also in foul shooting. Plus she's the Generalettes' tallest forward, almost as tall as Fritz Slappy. She's steady and smooth on the floor, fast—our second-fastest player. She steals the ball with a soft touch—

Oh, what difference does E.J. make? Or me? No one cares about our team. Another losing season coming up with a cretin coach! I socked my forehead.

I put my face on my desk and listened for the bell. How could I hear it over the pep rally next door in the cafeteria: "Lee High will shine tonight . . . shine tonight . . . shine tonight. . . ."

Rrrrring.

I decided to skip lunch. Who needs food power for jumping jacks? I could limber all season on one noodle. Sidestepping majorettes, banging my way through Lee's marching band, I headed for the gym. Classes never met there during a pep rally, I remembered from last year. I could practice foul shots in the—dark

And cold on court. My breath must be frosty, if I could only see it. My teeth began to chatter. Warm up, I told myself. And not with icky toe-touching. I fumbled along the sidelines in the dim light coming from under Coach O'Hara's office door. I trotted and swung my arms. I jogged and pumped my arms. I ran fast, faster, pumped harder. Up and down the gym until my foot touched a blob—a ball. Needs air. Must be brown, I thought. One of the girls' duds. I strained my eyes for the free-throw line. Right next to me I made out a wall with no bleachers. Must be the court's north end. I paced off steps to where I hoped the backboard would be. I looked up and saw it. I paced fifteen feet straight ahead, knelt down, and felt the free-throw line, slick paint on top of wood. I took my position there. I shot the blob. I listened for a swish. Instead I heard plop. Then I heard click. Click click.

Suddenly the gym was brilliant with light. I blinked and saw the net hanging still. So I'd missed! I saw where my ball had landed against the bleachers, right near some big feet in black tennis shoes . . . legs in gray sweat pants . . . arms in a Generals jacket . . . thick neck with a whistle hanging there . . . square jaw . . . tinted glasses . . . blue-and-gray baseball cap . . . scowling Coach Michael O'Hara. He said, "Free throws, I presume."

"Yes, sir."

"Then you might as well shoot them right."

In one fluid motion, he reached under the bleachers, palmed a ball, and passed it slap into my breadbasket. I didn't look down. I knew that ball was red-white-and-blue. It wrecked my stomach. "OOOOOOf."

"A good foul shooter should make seventy-five percent of his—her—tries from this line. Seventy-five out of a hundred. Seven hundred fifty out of a thousand. Seventy-five thousand out of a hundred thousand. Start keeping your score immediately."

Under Coach's scrutiny, I shot zero for ten. I mumbled, "Must be my dumb cold hands."

"Keep shooting," said Coach.

I shot one for ten. He retrieved my misses. He passed the ball back harder each time. His scowl never let up. His glasses caught the light and glared at me, too. Under his gaze I turned to jelly. "I'm nervous," I confessed, four out of thirty.

"You're improving," he said in his voice of iron. "And it's good to be nervous sometimes when you're practicing. You'll be nervous in games, especially near the end of close ones. Then free throws become crucial." He took off his cap. He growled, "Right now you're practicing under game conditions." He stared at me fiercely.

My hands trembled. Seven out of forty. My knees went numb. Ten out of fifty.

"Twenty percent," Coach said, holding my final miss. He came to the line. "The trick is to get into a groove that feels right. Practice and practice until you do the same things every time you stand here." He bounced the ball. "The referee hands you a ball. You take a deep breath, bounce the ball several times to get the feel. Look at the basket. Concentrate. Shut out noise from the crowd."

"What crowd?" I asked. "No one ever comes to girls' games except Aileen's boyfriend and my mother."

Coach ignored me. He bounced the ball again, took a breath, stared at the basket, paused, and let fly with a one-hand shot that swished. I dashed for the ball while he called "I notice that you shoot underhand with two hands. Nothing wrong with that style. Whatever *feels* right to you. Using two hands provides good control."

He shot again. I held up one finger for his point, the way his Generals do. He shot again. And again. Five times. I held up five fingers.

"Most close basketball games are decided at this free-throw line," he said and threw me the ball, harder than before. "You should practice every chance you get, especially when you're tired. Tiredness is a game condition—of the final quarter. Of overtime." He started briskly toward his office.

Girls' games never go into overtime, I almost called after him. But didn't. And I didn't ask him where I could practice, now that snow covered Arlington County's two outside courts. I knew he wouldn't volunteer this gym. No way! Not when his Generals needed it most of the time.

But not during pep rallies. I stayed at the line. I shot until my wrists ached. Fifty out of two hundred. I shot until Randy's socks were sopped. Ninety-five out of three hundred. I shot until my arms felt paralyzed and dangled at my sides. I'll never shoot again, I vowed, and shot one hundred for three hundred five. I knew I could never shoot five in a row again. But I did. On my way to one hundred fifty out of four hundred. Whew!

I kept track of my baskets, but not of time. When the bell rang, I knew I'd be late to math class. Okay, at least I had a ruler today. I grabbed my books and tape. My arm muscles yelled for a vacation but my legs felt super. I ran to math and later to history and still later to study hall, where Rinehart greeted me with carbohydrates—a briefcase full of "prescription" pancakes he'd made on his Bunsen burner. "Eat for Plan A," he said.

"Taste like radishes—ech—raw in the middle." I ate anyway. I knew I was goners without Rinehart's scheme. I wanted to be ready for it, whatever.

He worked on his log. He drew pictures with his ballpoint and added up rows of numbers. On another page he sketched a basketball play filled with X's and O's. He muttered to himself about footwork, shooting range, scoop passing, and stutter moves. I listened and watched instead of studying. He whispered, "If this doesn't work, we'll try the *other* court." He doodled a block **Z** on top of a page covered with ink already. "Alternate Plan Z," he said as we left for the gym. Rinehart ran ahead to plant himself under the bleachers.

Z? I asked myself.

Mrs. Butor was already on court wearing strange sneakers with pointy toes. Her baggy shorts caught the breeze each time she shuffled sideways in our warm-up trot. Her whistle bounced on her chest. After we'd limbered, she divided us into two rows for passing practice. She read directions aloud from *Official Guide to Girls' Basketball* and sat down to correct us. "Easier, easier, Suzanne," she called from her lounge.

I remembered Coach O'Hara's zippy throws at noon. I passed harder.

We switched to dribbling.

Mrs. Butor soon shouted at me for "unnecessary roughness," although I was nowhere near another Generalette. "The ball, Suzanne. You're mauling the ball." She gathered us around her at the foul circle. "You know, gals, when I was your age, the rules were so very different." She riffled pages of her *Guide*. "For example, we were not allowed to dribble. We could take only two bounces; then we had to pass or shoot." She grinned a nonstop grin. "Dribbling has always seemed so new-fashioned—so aggressive to me."

We switched to rebounding.

Joan, Putt, E.J., and Teeny shot baskets. Millie, Phyllis, JoJo, and Aileen tried to clear the boards. No contest! Tall E.J. won every time. She tapped misses for two points. Or she glided down holding the ball high and away. "No fair—fair." Aileen hissed loud enough for Mrs. Butor to send in short me as substitute. I out-positioned Phyllis on the first jump. We tangled going up and she came down with a crunch. I out-psyched Aileen on the second. We didn't jump. I rebounded alone after I kidded her about a certain ankle bracelet. "Unfair, Suzanne," Mrs. Butor warned. "And your body contact must cease."

We switched to defense.

"Dee-fense. Dee-fense. Dee-fense," I hollered to my teammates on court. I'd been benched already for "tussling." I'd joggled the ball loose from Millie's catch at the center jump. So there I sat, a solo pep squad. I shouted, "Press, press. Don't give 'em a break. Take 'em in the corners and smother their shooting. Watchit. Watchit. Good move, E.J. Put the clamps on. Tighter—"

"Silence, Suzanne. I am the Generalettes' coach."

"But Mrs. Butor, they're mostly playing pitty-pat out there."

"Suzanne. I wish you would stop being difficult." She huffed that.

"I haven't *started* being difficult," I answered, looking under the bleachers for Rinehart's help. I had no plan of my own except to sit and mourn a lot.

But I wasn't going to need a plan because at that very moment when Mrs. Butor seemed ready to banish me to a season-long shower, Rinehart stepped between us. He turned to her and said in the sweetest of voices, "Mrs. Butor, I couldn't stay away from this gym when I heard of your dedication to basketball." He smiled his brightest smile, the one he usually saved for his pet newt. He put down his briefcase and shook Butor's hand. "I am Arthur Rinehart, student in this building. As a scientist I would like to collect some valuable statistics for my next Arlington County Science Fair project. You may well recall I have won first prize several years now." Rinehart made *several* sound like forever.

Mrs. Butor seemed to remember something about Rinehart. At least she didn't back away from him.

Rinehart cleared his throat. "I was wondering if you would be willing to test your, er, acclaimed method of coaching the Generalettes against my, er, experimental method." He pulled out an *Official Guide to Boys' Basketball* from his briefcase.

Now Mrs. Butor backed away.

Rinehart smiled reassuringly. "Rules and techniques of play described in my book and in yours are rather alike these days."

Mrs. Butor gasped, "I should hope not."

"Of course, of course," Rinehart sympathized. "And therein lies my experiment." He hurried his sentences, almost as if he didn't want Mrs. Butor to understand any words but the ones he came down hard on. "I would like to measure the *wisdom*—the *effectiveness*—of *your* coaching method against this, er, *newfangled* method." He waved his *Guide* gently. Marked-up pages fluttered around him. "This body-contact method versus your *restrained* but *winning* basketball."

Mrs. Butor couldn't seem to follow Rinehart's request. She gazed from his *Guide* to his slipping glasses to the hideous maroon tie he'd worn for Plan A.

"Thus science would discover once and for all if girls are equal—"

"Arthur, what would the experiment involve?" She backed away further.

"Nothing that would upset your regular basketball practice, I assure you, Mrs. Butor."

She looked disappointed.

"I would need to borrow two players to use as guinea pigs. Suzanne perhaps."

Mrs. Butor grinned again.

"Yes, perhaps Suzanne would do."

Perhaps nothing. He'd better take me, I thought.

"And Eleanor Johnston. I will train them for eight days while you coach your followers. Then I will measure the basketball abilities of each girl. I fully expect your Generalettes to score considerably higher than—"

"A superb experiment, Arthur. It should win you first prize. Suzanne, Eleanor, report to Mr. Rinehart at the far end of the gym. Aileen, Pauletta—everyone else—join me in warming up again after this long interruption."

Rinehart sluffed off his overcoat, rolled up his sleeves, and said, "Man-on-man scrimmage." He fed us the ball.

I said, "Arthur, you mean well."

Swish.

"No I don't."

Chapter 4

BASKETBALL PRACTICE SCHEDULE

To: E.J. Johnston and Z. Hagen
Date: Thursday, January 5th
Coach: A. Rinehart

3:00-3:10	Free-Throw Shooting (Buddy System)
3:10-3:15	Dribbling Drill
3:15-3:20	40 Passes Each: 10 bounce; 10 chest; 10 overhand; 10 underhand
3:20-3:25	Full-speed lay-up shooting
3:25-3:30	Rebound Drill
3:30-3:40	Mano a Mano
3:40-3:45	Spot shooting from at least 20 feet out
3:45-4:15	Suicide Running

NOTES AND COMMENTS

Zan: Remember that at the free-throw line, your height doesn't matter. Here all players are equal. Stop grumbling about being short.

E.J.: Use your height in going for rebounds. Stretch for extra inches. Develop skill as a tipper. Throw the ball against the board, leap, and tip the ball into the basket with your right hand. Repeat drill with your left hand.

Zan: Don't slap the ball when you're dribbling. Don't watch the ball. Keep your head and eyes up. Dribble with your fingertips. Watch the person who is guarding you (either me or E.J.).

E.J.: Improve your jump shot by letting go of the ball at the top of your jump, not on your way down.

Both: In one-on-one practice, fake one way, fake another, fake a lay-up or a jump shot, move your shoulder, move your eyes--do anything to get your guard going the wrong way. Then zip around her.

Both: Even though the Generals take over the court at 3:45, you both can use the out-of-bounds lines to run around for ½ hour. Run at top speed until completely winded. Ease off and jog while you count 60. Then run at top speed, etc. Run until your lungs ache and your tongue goes dry. In this way you will build up your wind.

Chapter 5

"Rinehart, tomorrow's the day," I reminded him with my last gasp of air.

"You are both ready," Rinehart panted. His white breath seemed like explosions of confidence. He held his earmuffs and sprinted with us a last lap around the football goalposts. "You will win every test."

All week, during study hall, we'd been suicide-running our favorite field. Rinehart had forged absentee excuses for the three of us. He could write the same as anyone's father. He'd given us weird diseases with Latin names and promised that if we skipped studying and ran hard, we'd blow the Generalettes right off the court. Every indoor session, he produced a fresh set of passes to pass, shots to shoot, drills to drill while he chased rebounds or checked his stopwatch or read aloud from books about professional basketball. We looked at pictures and imitated the all-stars. We hustled every second of Rinehart's practice. Then we ran suicides an extra thirty minutes in company with the Generals, who were warming up for their two-hour scrimmages.

Most of the boys never noticed us. To them we might as well have been invisible. But Fritz tossed an elbow in my ribs every time I came close, and Randy yelled "El Freako" as he passed me. He whispered worse if I passed him. When Coach O'Hara blew his whistle, we freaks left his gym for our locker room.

Where we'd crumble on benches, too tired for showers. We'd watch ourselves dying in the mirrors. We'd listen to our hearts thumping. When they'd gone quiet as the faucets dripping, I'd try to stand up. Down. No, up. I'm alive! Moaning, I'd haul myself off to get dressed. Oh, the muscle pain!

Generalettes were long gone. No one there but us cripples.

We'd been there on the weekend, too, through the window that I'd left unlatched late Friday afternoon. We climbed in at 7:00 A.M. Saturday, climbed out at 10:00 A.M., just ahead of the Boys' Midget League. We climbed in and out Sunday, too, just ahead of the Boys' Church League. In those six hours we'd hooked and jumped and layed up a trillion shots. We'd run a zillion times around the cold gym. We'd huffed and puffed at each other in the mano-a-mano drills. Rinehart helped E.J. guard me. "Double-team the eel," he'd cry. "She'll give us the slip again."

I'd fake right, I'd go left and do it. I'd score because Arthur Rinehart couldn't guard a stop sign. Plus E.J. was bushed.

"My arms feel heavier than aircraft carriers," she'd say when I held up two fingers.

"My tongue's dragging the boards," I'd confess.

"Perfect!" announced Rinehart. "Now's the precise time for free-throw practice. Now under game conditions. Remember to shoot a little harder to compensate for your loss of power from being overtired."

"We're totaled, Rinehart, not tired."

Totaled or not, I shot. Two hundred fifty out of

seven hundred. Three hundred out of eight hundred twenty.

E.J. slumped against the wall. She had long since hit seventy-five percent of her foul shots. I'd seen her sink seventeen in a row. I'd tossed back her rebounds the day she shot twenty-four out of twenty-five. Steady, smooth E.J. sitting there in a pool of sweat, eyes closed in exhaustion.

Swish. Slap. Bounce. Slap, bounce, thud. Swish. Slap kerplop. Kerplop. Slap. Swish.

E.J. said quietly, "You're getting there." She'd been listening to my shots.

I told her, "You're the one with the magic touch." I counted three hundred six out of eight hundred twenty-nine.

"No magic. I practiced at camp every day for seven summers."

Rinehart caught my final swish and whispered, "Here comes the church league bus." We escaped to our locker room and out the window. With a final burst of carbohydrates, I sprinted across the football field, E.J. swift behind me. Rinehart called, "Wait up. You've earned a rest."

"He really knows how to treat a girl," I groaned to E.J.

"Uh huh. Like boys," she said with her second, third, or fourth wind.

"Our day has come," I announced to Rinehart on that Friday, the thirteenth. "We'll win your experiment for sure."

I was dressed in my cleanest sweats and raring to

score. My new Keds hugged the floorboards. They fit me just right. Rinehart had seen to that. He'd paid for them, too, out of earnings from *Rinehart's Science Newsletter.* He felt his gift was fair because he planned to write about me and E.J. in the next issue: "The Effects of Boys' Basketball Techniques Upon Selected Girls at Robert E. Lee Junior-Senior High School." He gave E.J. some blue-and-gray sweatbands for her wrists and three quarts of Gatorade.

She sipped some now, watching the Generalettes limber up. Except for flying basketballs, their end of Lee gym looked like the main deck of an ocean liner. Players wore tennis dresses stitched with their maroon names, tiny on the collar. Aileen. Mildred. JoAnne. If I squinted, I could read from the foul circle. They also wore pink socks and matching bloomers that showed when they rebounded. They mainly didn't jump. They avoided jostling for possession. They passed slowly, deliberately. No one seemed to sweat. No one hollered.

"Gals, gals, gals." Mrs. Butor brought the contest to order.

"Listen," I shouted to my one teammate. E.J. joined me in the crowd around a table that Rinehart had placed on the sidelines. From here he would reign as judge.

He spoke rapidly, outlining his rules. He pointed to strips of black tape on the court—spots to stand on, lines to cross or not to cross. He pointed to green starting lines and red finish lines. He wound his stopwatch and set it at zero. He laid out his log. He wished everyone good luck. He licked his pencil. He said, "Play ball."

We began with suicide laps, us against them. Within a minute, half the Generalettes dropped out. In another minute, E.J. and I galloped alone. The rest held their sides, gasping.

"Stamina," called Rinehart. "Ten points to my players."

We lined up again, us against the field. We ran a quarter mile—five laps around the out-of-bounds markings. I finished first, E.J. second, Joan and Millie finished finally. No one else crossed the red line.

"Speed," called Rinehart. "Ten points to the sweat shirts."

"Wretched sweat shirts," I heard Mrs. Butor snap to Aileen.

Rinehart put down his pencil. He motioned for Teeny's help. Together they carried folding chairs on court and arranged them down the middle. "These are guards, twelve feet apart," Rinehart instructed us. "Your task is to dribble in and out of these eight chairs, from one end of the floor to the other. Starting with Teeny. Take your marks, set, go."

The Generalettes maneuvered slowly among the chairs, careful not to touch them. Aileen's curls stayed plastered to her head. JoJo's bloomers stayed hidden. Everyone smiled at one another as if she were winning.

"That's it, gals! One smiles as one competes. Like ice skating."

"No. No. No. That will never do," Rinehart answered their coach, exasperated. "I'm testing their agility *and* speed. They must sprint this course, keeping their eyes on the chairs and off the ball.

Facial expressions don't count. My stopwatch does the counting. Get set—go."

Racing the course now, every Generalette made mistakes. Polly collided with four chairs going, five coming. Putt lost her ball when it hit a rung and bounded under the bleachers. Phyllis bashed her shin on number 7 guard. Nat wouldn't leave the chair she sat on.

Rinehart signaled E.J. to her mark. With a click of his watch, she dribbled off the green tape. She swept through the chairs. Her moves were easy and fluid. At the red tape, she lobbed me the basketball. I didn't smile. I eyed the chairs as enemies. I took off hard. I wove among my guards. I bumped number 4 and crunched number 7 but never missed a beat.

"Ten points to my agile speedsters," called Rinehart, toasting us with a bottle of Gatorade. We chugalugged beside our coach. We swiped our brows on each other's backs. Revived, we met Rinehart's further tests.

"Alertness. Ten points to E.J. and Zan."

"Suzanne. Please avoid flustering my gals."

"Rebounding. Ten more to the grabbers."

"You're rumpling my uniform," Aileen complained.

Rinehart called, "Full-speed lay-ups now. Sprint and shoot from the right side. Break left to the black tape. Sprint and shoot from the left side. As many baskets as you can make in sixty seconds. Accuracy and speed both count. Take your marks."

"Arthur, would you allow my gals to refresh themselves in the bleachers? They seem fatigued."

"Mrs. Butor, I beg you. Your Generalettes must

finish these trials before the Generals take over the court. If we stop, I can only assume that your gals—how shall I say? Their team morale is questionable."

"Gals, toe your marks."

They toed and we won. Then Rinehart lined us up for floor shots. "Shoot two from this spot, two from that spot, and so on. Ten shots each. Polly, begin."

Polly made four. Her twin, Teeny, made four. Nat bagged five. Joan hit one out of eight before she quit in disgust. Busy smoothening her tennis dress, Aileen didn't take her turn. E.J. did. She swished nine for ten. I followed her lead. I set my feet carefully on the tapes. I drew deep breaths. I put extra stuff on the ball because I was tired. I shot eight for ten, two of these from way back court.

Rinehart lit the scoreboard with details of our victory so far. HOME O VISITORS 70. He waved at the near wall. "You will notice a target conveniently close. Stand on this tape and pass for that target. Two chest passes. Two bounce passes. Two hooks. Two overhand, two underhand."

This time E.J. led off. Hook—bull's-eye. Overhand, bounce, chest, underhand—bull's-eye. "Great fun," she said, turning the ball over to Bumpy.

"No it's not. I'm falling-down tired," Bumpy said back crossly.

"You rest up. I'll go next," I offered, relieving her of the burdensome Wilson basketball. I cocked my wrists. I bounced a beaut on target. SSSSSmack. Another SSSSSmack. I fired my overhands faster than usual.

"Why so hard, Suzanne? Such foul play isn't necessary."

"Why?" I asked my ex-coach, who watched me with a shiver. "These would be tough for our enemies to intercept." SSSSSmack. "Admiralettes could never pick them off."

With my seventh pass, the target crashed down. Rinehart rushed to rehang it but couldn't make the frayed edges stay firm. While he stapled and tacked and taped, Mrs. Butor yelled at him about my "aggressive tendencies" and my "dismaying pushiness." "She bangs into these poor gals. She'd ruin my team—any team she played on."

Pretty soon Rinehart saluted her with his hammer. "Mrs. Butor, for your sake I shall drop passing accuracy as a measure of basketball performance." He crumpled the fallen target. He adjusted his maroon tie. "We'll progress directly to the mano-a-mano event."

I whispered, "Lucky for us Mrs. Butor doesn't know Spanish. She'd nail her Generalettes' feet to the floor before she'd let them go man against man."

Rinehart gave instructions. "Mano against ette, so to speak. My players challenge your players, one at a time. Joan, you and Nat, Teeny, Polly, and Aileen—line up and wait your turn at Zan. You five others line up down there to wait your shot at E.J."

I noticed that Rinehart had matched me against the shorties. "Good thinking," I told my coach. Tall E.J. winked as she took her position.

Rinehart continued. "Zan starts with the ball at half-court. She must score against Joan within thirty seconds. Then Joan tries scoring against Zan. The important skill here is moves. You all can twist, pivot, feint, slip right or left, leap straight ahead, flow, soar for the basket."

Mrs. Butor looked slightly less sulky. "Rather like dancing, the way you describe it, Arthur."

Not quite dancing! I broke from the center circle at the click of Rinehart's watch. I didn't twist or flow or soar. I dribbled straight for Joan, who stationed herself thirty feet from the backboard. I arrived at my guard. She raised her arms. I faked right. She followed. I faked right again. She followed. I left her there off-balance and seething. I drove for a lay-up and sank it.

As we walked to center court for Joan's whack at me, I watched E.J. go one-on-one with Millie. They confronted each other at the foul circle. E.J. had managed to bring the ball to her favorite spot. Now to shake off her guard. She dribbled in place. Millie lowered her hands, trying to snatch the ball on its upward bounce. She missed it. E.J. caught the ball, and, in the split second before Millie upped her arms to block a shot, E.J. whooshed forward. She let fly. Slap, kerplop through the net.

Mano after mano, everything broke our way. I wiped out Nat. E.J. dusted off Bumpy and JoJo. I shook free of Teeny and Polly. E.J. scored again from her spot. Next she put the right fakes on Putt while I waited for Aileen to uncrinkle her collar.

"Go," Rinehart kept saying.

Aileen flounced toward my outstretched arms. I reached to knock the ball loose. "Meanie," she said.

I dropped my hands. "It's just part of the game, Aileen." I started to say I'm sorry, but right in there she tossed the ball over my surprised head.

Was her shot high enough? Long enough?

Neither.

I picked off the rebound. I bounced the Wilson, listening for Rinehart's stopwatch to click.

Click. "Go."

I tried to get off the line. Aileen stuck to me like a dancing partner. I dribbled to my left, shielding the ball with my body. Aileen dug at it with her fingernails—pushed it beyond my reach. For a second I watched the black letters spin away.

"Hang tough," I told myself. I ducked Aileen's claws. I broke for the foul circle, dived for the ball. With it safe in the crook of one arm, I burst to my feet again, only to find myself eyelash to eyelash with Aileen. I couldn't squirm past. My thirty seconds must be almost up. I'd have to fake—no—I'd have to shove—there! I shoved Mrs. Butor's favorite and shot for two points.

"Time's up," called Rinehart. "Ten more for the manos." He hailed us all to the table. "My final experiment next."

Groans.

"I suppose you will feel that this upcoming event will be an anticlimax after the more spectacular moments we have shared this afternoon." Rinehart looked from face to face, smiling beamishly. "Yet in your overly tired condition, perhaps a few gentle shots at the unattended basket would be as pleasurable as another boisterous duel."

Faces brightened, smiled back.

Smoothly Rinehart continued. "Therefore, Generalettes, take your places at the foul line. Shoot ten. I'll just jot your totals on my clipboard."

He jotted a lot of four for tens, five for tens. And presto, E.J.'s nine for ten. I waited last in line behind Aileen, who counted her misses aloud. "Faster, Aileen," I urged her, hearing Generals' voices behind their locker-room door. I also heard Coach O'Hara shouting his daily schedule.

"Boys, run twenty laps. Then we'll take jump-ball situations. Out-of-bounds drill. Fast breaking. Run through every special pattern including the freeze. Full-court press. Half-court sagging. Man-to-man defense. Foul shooting. Weight training. Steam room. Tonight, study your Generals' playbook, pages 80 to 85. You, Boyle, don't forget to tape your ankles. Cunningham, tighten that knee guard. Everyone be dressed and on court in one minute."

"Faster, Aileen." I scooped up her ball and fired it back.

"Uh nine misses. Uh ten."

"Aileen, zero for ten," Rinehart noted aloud. He pressed a button. HOME 0 VISITORS 85. "Zan, you're on."

I stepped to the line. I bounced the ball three times. I breathed sweaty air. I looked up at the basket. I shot one swisher. When E.J. returned the ball, I caught a look at Coach O'Hara out of the corner of my eye. He filled the locker-room doorway, muscular arms holding back his eager team. I heard Randy blurt, "Come on, Coach. Let us out on court."

I bounced the ball again. Breathed. Looked at the hoop. Shot. Swish.

Bounce. Breathe. Look. Shoot. Splat, Kerplunk. Three for three.

"Aw nuts. It's our turn," Fritz whined over Coach's shoulder.

Bounce. Breathe. Look. Shoot. Swish. Bounce. Breathe. Look. Shoot. Slap, slap, kerplop. Bounce, bounce, bounce. Look and look. Shoot harder. Swish. Bounce. Bounce. Bounce slower. Think. I will make this shot. I will make this shot under pressure.

"Nuts to that. Quit hogging the court!"

"Quiet or I'll bench you, Fritz Slappy." Coach's voice of iron.

Bounce. Bounce. Breathe deeper. Look longer. Shoot. Slap. Slap. Thud. In.

"Seven for seven." Rinehart made sure everyone heard. Silence from Generals and Generalettes.

Silence broken with the thwack of E.J.'s pass to my palms. Bounce. Bounce. Breathe some more. Look again. Shoot. Swish. Another "Nuts" from the locker-room doorway. Another "Quiet" from Coach O'Hara. Bounce. Concentrate. Breathe. Believe you can sink it. Look and believe. Shoot. Slapada. Slapada. Spin. Spinnnnnnn in.

"Nine for nine," proclaimed Rinehart in Coach O'Hara's direction. Silence from Coach. Not even a smile.

"Three hundred sixteen out of eight hundred thirty-nine," I corrected him. I'm finding the groove. I'm doing the exact same things over and over. Bounce. Breathe. Look at the target. Shut out the voices.

Randy called, "Miss it, ya retard."

His jeer shattered the gym's stale air. Bounce. His little green eyes found mine. Breathe deep. His words echoed in my head. Stare at the glass backboard, not at Randy. Don't clutch. Find the rim. It looks like it's in motion. Watch the basket. Make it stay still. Concentrate. Wrists up.

"Hey, choke, choke."

"Boyle, you're through for the day. Get out of uniform and go home—pronto."

Coach's command rang in my ear. Shoot up, I said to myself. Shoot. No, wait. Don't. Bounce it again. Think positive. Think about the game on Monday with the Admiralettes. Our first Generalettes game. No, wait. Bounce. Breathe and don't think. Look. Look and shoot harder. Follow through.

Is my shot high enough? Long enough?

Both.

"Ten for ten. Ten big ones." Rinehart hugged me and raced to the scoreboard switch. "How about that, Mrs. Butor?" She was nowhere to be seen. Or to see the score.

HOME 0 VISITORS 90

"Of course, my experiment called for one hundred points," Rinehart hollered over the Generals' stampede. They were running laps now, blue-and-gray streaks.

"You'll get those points next time," Coach O'Hara assured him. Then he fixed me with his steely eyes. "How would you like to scrimmage with my team today?"

Chapter 6

"How wouldja like a Wilson sandwich—smack in the old mouth?" Fritz Slappy asked me on the fifteenth lap. "That's whatcha gonna get if you hang around here today." His bony red elbow swung in my direction. I slowed to avoid a Fritz sandwich, but Eugene Matello caught me from behind. He stepped on my heel, jerked off my shoe. I stopped at the bleachers to put it back on.

"Pssssst, Zannie. I'm down here. I'll copy some ideas from O'Hara's scrimmage. I'll add them to my plans for your Monday game with the Admiral-ettes."

I couldn't answer Rinehart because Coach O'Hara's whistle brought us players to center court. I sort of stayed back from the circle of Generals. Fritz cracked his red knuckles and muttered, "Beat it." Eugene fierced his eyes. Monk Cunningham tucked in his shirt, adjusted the blue sweatband he wore around his forehead, and gave me the once-over. DumDum Cadden gazed off into space. He blew a gum bubble that popped at Fritz's nose. Everyone laughed except Coach. And me. I wasn't exactly quaking in my sneakers, but I wasn't feeling jokey, either. I knew I was about to get a mouthful of their red-white-and-blue ball. Sooner or later I'd also catch Monk's St. Christopher medal cold in my teeth. And swallow Ben Brown's flapping jersey. And choke on

Eugene's long black hair. A menu full of Generals, coming up!

Coach O'Hara twirled his whistle on its lanyard, expecting quiet. He didn't need to wait long. He said, "Boys, our season will be a disaster if you continue to play as individuals. You must work together." He watched for *together* to sink in. He switched the ball from hand to hand, saying "Teamwork. Teamwork."

Fritz shrugged. DumDum puffed another bubble. Eugene shot savage looks all around himself—not just at me. Monk nibbled the chain of his medal. Ben Brown kept his eyes on the floor.

"And teamwork starts with the tip-off." Coach gave his bullet stare to each player. "Boys, you will practice jumping for the ball right here. Take your places in the circle—Slappy against Cadden, five jumps. First stringers, spread out and reach for Slappy's tip. He will look for you and aim at a teammate. You—second stringers—you intercept."

Coach tossed the basketball straight up. Fritz tipped it once, twice, three times—every time.

"Jump, DumDum, jump," Monk Cunningham called. But DumDum's big feet hardly moved an inch.

"Use your height. Don't just stand there flat-footed," I couldn't help saying. For an answer, DumDum blew his biggest bubble, round as his head.

Left of me, Eugene caught all of Fritz's tips. They worked together as a two-man team, shutting the other first stringers out. Up Fritz; tap to Eugene. Up, tap, down, Eugene. Monk leapt futilely after the ball. Ben Brown reached twice and gave up.

Now Eugene tapped to Fritz, tapped to Fritz three

more times. "Two guys isn't teamwork," I said, hoping to rally the second stringers. I coiled further down, sprang a little higher each tap. I semi squatted. I came up in my highest leap. All I got for that jump was a shoulder in my ear.

"You and you—Matello against Cunningham. And boys, for the fullest possible extension of your bodies, go up one-handed. Try to flick the ball with your wrist. Don't sock. Don't swat it." Coach tossed the jump-ball high. Monk flicked it to Ben Brown. Monk up, flick to Fritz. Up, flick to DumDum, who seemed amazed by his catch. He almost swallowed his gum.

"I dunno how I caught it." DumDum laughed with the whole squad.

Coach explained. "Cunningham flicked it to you, and you had position. You stood in your guard's way and muscled him out. Get ready to do that again."

"I dunno if I can."

"For sure you can," I whispered to him.

"I dunno—"

"You're a deep one, Cadden," Fritz snarled and cocked his elbows.

Coach's toss was too low and crooked. He caught it himself, saying "No two referees throw the ball to the same height. Some don't even throw it straight. Over this season, we'll study the refs in our league. We'll keep track of their styles. We'll adapt to them. Ready."

I got ready. Monk might flick to me since he'd been taking turns. I edged between DumDum and Fritz. I crouched. When the ball went up, they went up. I went up slower, lower. Monk tipped the ball down hard, right into my mitts. I hung on for dear life. A surly silence collected around me, broken only by Coach's "Zan, the ball. Zan Hagen." I forked it over but I still felt its sting on my fingertips.

Ah.

I coiled for Monk's last jump. He looked down at me with serious blue eyes. He looked over my shoulder. I started to move with the toss. Fritz and Dum-Dum clashed in midair while I squirmed backwards after the ball. Monk had tipped it high and hard over everyone's head. To me!

Generals growled at Monk, but Coach told him, "Fine teamwork. Good strategy. Surprise is always effective, Cunningham. And you, Zan, good position." Coach met my grin. He seemed to notice me for the second time. He barked, "Zan against Brown." He took the ball from me with one sure hand. He used his other hand to draw me into the circle by my sleeve. I peeked up at Ben through my soaking bangs. No way I would ever out-jump our tallest player.

No way.

To ace me out, Ben Brown hardly had to lift his feet off the boards. He tapped to Monk, to Monk, to Monk twice more. Fritz and Eugene were laughing, both shaking so hard they couldn't catch the ball. Coach tossed number 5, 6, 7, number 8. "You'll jump until you tap one, Hagen," he bellowed and put number 9 up above my head. I reached in an explosion of energy and missed. I coiled, sprang, missed, crouched, sprang on 11. I bent just a little, re-resprang. Number 12 was tipped by Ben. And 13. I stared up at him. I coughed deep in my throat. I asked, "Ben, do you want a knuckle sandwich?" Ben looked down in disbelief, the ball went up, and I tipped number 14 to Monk.

Ben hollered, "That doesn't count. The, uh, lady distracted me."

" 'Course it counts. She psyched you out. Fine strategy." Coach nodded with satisfaction.

Fritz hissed, "Big creeping deal. She couldn't do it again."

"Don't be too sure," Monk answered him. Quietly.

Coach motioned for the ball. "She only has to do it once—that's what psyching out is all about." He looked down at me. "I've got an idea for our game tomorrow night. We'll let our shortest player take the center jump. That ought to confuse the Admirals, make them wonder what we're up to. Not one of you can outjump their pivot man anyway." He glowered at Ben. "Brown, you're taller but their Vanderkallen's never lost a tip to you in three years."

Ben bowed his head.

"Then who's gonna take the center jump—this girl?" Fritz pretended to lob me a ball. Laughter rippled around the team, egging him on. "She oughtta psych out the Admirals. Wait'll I tell Randy, you guys."

The laughing stopped at Coach O'Hara. He never even cracked his lips. He glanced down at me, all sweaty and out of place in his ring of big Generals. He said, "No, not Zan. She hasn't practiced with us. She doesn't know your moves or shooting spots. She hasn't memorized our playbook." Coach didn't mention my height. He didn't say *girl* or *lady*. Instead he announced, as if it were final, "Without scrimmaging as a General—without studying our set plays—she'd be at a loss anywhere except on the foul line."

"And in the center circle," Monk reminded Coach. Monk opened his mouth to say more, but Fritz gave him a shove.

Monk didn't push back. He picked up a basketball and began taking set shots by himself. After the first three swishers from twenty feet out, I planted myself under the basket to save Monk time. I put extra spin on my passes so he wouldn't think I was used to throwing cotton candy. He didn't say "Ouch" or anything.

Everyone else seemed to be shouting, pushing and pulling each other, joking around. Then Jumbo Williams kicked Eugene Matello from behind. Eugene whirled to fight back. He punched Ben, who ducked and dove away. He tried to punch Fritz, but Fritz ran faster around the sidelines. Plus Fritz had breath left over to holler "Nuts to you, Matello. Beat up on the Admirals, not on me. Or Randy'll get you."

Coach O'Hara moved to the portable blackboard he'd set up near the bleachers. He drew a diagram and called, "Team and substitutes to the sidelines."

I got there first. I heard scuttling under the bleachers—Rinehart finding a better seat for our lesson. "I've heard everything, Zanner," he whispered to let me know where.

While the team gathered near him, Coach O'Hara printed OUT-OF-BOUNDS PLAY under his diagram. He said, "When we put the ball into play from the sidelines, we'll score with this." He paused to glare at his quarreling Generals. He labeled the X's and O's on the board with each guy's name until he came to MATELLO. He said, "Matello, you're one reason we're losing this season. You're a hothead. You waste time fighting when you should be working with your own team. And you, Slappy!" Coach rubbed his name from the board. "Slappy, you call yourself a leader? You're supposed to take over as captain if Boyle's not on the floor. Teamwork takes leadership! Brown, you allow these boys—and every boy in our league—to bully you." Coach erased Ben's name. "Cadden, do you ever plan to study your playbook? The only move you've learned this season is romping with your bubble gum!"

"Aw, Coach." DumDum watched his name disappear.

Coach ignored every mumble and hurt look from his cutups. He printed TEAMWORK TEAMWORK TEAMWORK where he'd erased their names. Then he said, "You all should know this play already. Take your assigned spots on court."

I didn't ask my place. I was certain Coach would erase me—never mind my name—if he happened to notice I still hung around. I stayed in the bleachers trying to figure out where I might belong in his out-of-bounds play: maybe right where I sat, way, way out-of-bounds. For good.

"Psssst, Zan. Go in and guard Eugene. He's your man, I figured out." Rinehart poked me with his ballpoint.

"Find the free man," Coach called to the Generals. "Matello. Hit him, he's free."

Not for long, I thought, coming off the bench and into action. I tore like a demon up the middle. Matello, with his back to my position, couldn't see me until he turned to break away for a pass. He drove into me. He whammed me so hard that I lay there wondering what court I was on. Lee's? Swanson's? Washington Coliseum?

"Foul! Foul!" yelped Rinehart from under the stands.

"I don't call violations during practice." Coach collared Rinehart. "Might as well come out so you can research all the action, Arthur."

They sat together in the bleachers, watching Ben help me stand up. My legs felt teetery but I said "Okay" when Monk asked "Okay?" We took our positions again and practiced the same play two dozen times. Coach didn't yell "Hit Matello," because Eugene never got free. I stayed pasted to him every direction he broke. He broke slow, is why. His mouth gaped, his arms swayed useless at his sides. He was tired. Worse off than me with my ringing ears.

Ten minutes later, Coach reorganized us into fast-break teams. Four on three, three on two, two on one, we swarmed the basket. "Hit the open man," Coach shouted and clapped for the pinpoint passes, the improving lay-ups. I ran hard. I kept up. I ran past. I was usually open, never hit. No General threw me the ball. O'Hara tapped his playbook against his knee for emphasis. "Keep your head high while you dribble." He waved his chalk like a wand. "Breakers, get the rebound. Be alive. Help each other. Matello, run! Slappy, feed Brown at the post. Cunningham, fake a shot and pass off to another breaker. Hit the open—"

"Ette," yelled Rinehart. "Hit the Generalette."

Fritz hit Monk, Monk hit DumDum, DumDum hit Eugene.

"I'm open—I'm free," I told the team.

Eugene hit Jumbo, Jumbo hit Ben. Over and over.

No one hit me except with a hip under the basket. Once I caught a flying finger between my eyes. And a shot in my ribs. Things got pretty pushy around the old hoop.

"Go into your freeze now, boys." Coach held up three fingers. "Try a three-minute stall."

I wondered what he could mean. Freeze? Stall? Us Generalettes hadn't learned a freeze or any of these plays. Never mind. I'd teach every move to our team on Monday. I'd use the same portable blackboard—same court—before our first game.

Alongside me, the first stringers dribbled and passed, stood still and passed, dribbled, cut, and passed, passed and cut, cut and caught and dribbled and passed. Not one guy shot the ball. Not star Fritz when he got open. Not guard Monk from his favorite spot back court. Not Ben from his high-post position. Not Eugene with his exhausted hands he could hardly unclench. All they did was pass and cut. Cut and pass. Fritz to Eugene to Ben to Fritz to Eugene to Monk to Fritz to Eugene to Ben to Monk to Eugene to Fritz to—

Wheeeeet. Coach gave a mighty blast on his whistle. "Boys, come with me to the blackboard."

On the sidelines, each player toweled off and flopped down. Fritz put on his warm-up jacket. Ben sucked an orange. Eugene squirted water down his throat from a plastic bottle. My own stolen towel had disappeared, no doubt into Rinehart's briefcase. Our Gatorade went home with E.J. I leaned against the blackboard, parched and useless. That whole long freeze and I'd never so much as touched the ball. It must have been a freeze on me.

"Down in front," nagged Fritz. "We wanna see the picture."

I dropped between Jumbo and Eugene. They moved way over. Behind me, Monk whispered, "You okay?"

"Okay." But I wasn't. I needed a sip of water. I needed to feel the basketball again.

"Whyncha give up, girl?" Fritz's favorite question.

"Yeah," DumDum agreed.

"Boys, review this freeze with me." The *yeahs* went no further. Every eye fastened on Coach's flying chalk.

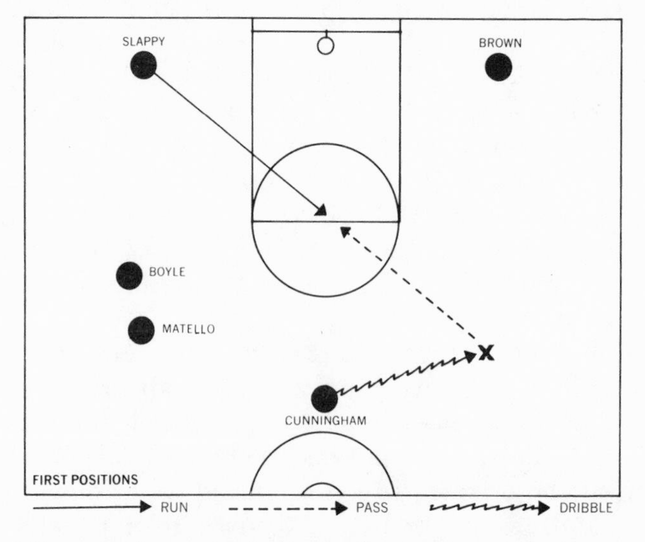

"Cunningham, with the ball, starts our freeze pattern. He gives a signal—three fingers held high. He dribbles to his right. To this X. At the same time,

Slappy will run to the foul line. Cunningham passes to Slappy. A crisp pass. No floaters in the freeze."

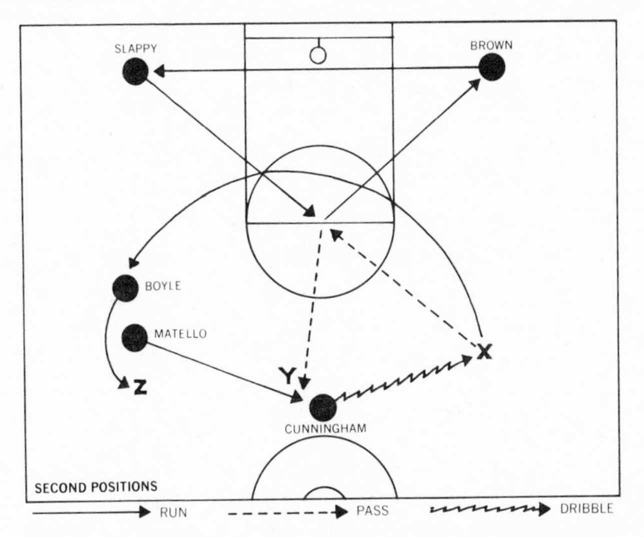

"Slappy next passes to Matello, who's moved fast from his original position. Here, at this Y. Notice what happens to Slappy and Brown. They rotate positions, over and over. Right corner to left corner. Left corner to foul line. Foul line to right corner. Right corner to left corner, and so forth." He sketched their moves. "One of the two players receives the ball every other pass. Brown or Slappy."

I followed Coach's lines, hoping to see my own name. Or even my initial, somewhere in all those capital letters.

"Boys, this simple pattern will save games for us, no doubt about that. When we're ahead in the final minutes, we'll freeze the ball so our opponents can't score. They'll have to foul us to get possession."

"That means curtains for the Admirals, the Wolfmen, the Warriors," Fritz predicted.

"No, not unless you improve your team foul-shooting. Only Boyle and Cunningham hit a dependable percentage." Coach looked squarely at us all. "And Zan—her average has improved tremendously. Learn her secret, boys. It's called practice, practice, practice."

Fritz hooted. "Us? Learn from her?" He thumped Eugene who thumped DumDum who thumped Monk. The thumps stopped there. Monk handed me the water bottle.

Coach struck the blackboard with his knuckles. "And you must practice this freeze again. Pass sharp. Catch clean. Move fast to your next position. Cunningham runs from this X over to Boyle's spot. Matello has already run to this Y position to catch Slappy's pass. Catch and dribble, Matello. To this X and pass. Then follow this line over to Boyle's spot." Coach drew a long curved arrow ending at Randy's last name. "Boyle has already run to this—"

Fritz interrupted. "Who's freezing for Randy today?"

"To this **Z**," Coach continued, making a block letter to emphasize his words. "Zan's subbing for Boyle. And throw her the ball. She can catch. She'll throw it back, don't worry. Help each other. Run the freeze again and help each other."

We set up in Coach's formation. The ball made its circuit: Monk Cunningham to Fritz Slappy to Eugene Matello to Ben Brown to—never to me. The second stringers, playing defense, chased the varsity, chased the basketball, then got frustrated and started fouling all over the court. Really fouling! Slaps sounded like train wrecks. Elbows must have felt like ramrods. Fists must have tasted scabby. But how would I know? I wasn't fouled because I didn't get near the ball.

"Hey, this isn't keep-away," I finally hollered from my spots. "Throw me the ball. Or at least foul me. Here, right in the old mouth." I bared my teeth.

"Kiss off," called Fritz.

Generals fought harder. Tripping. Spearing. Jabbing. In the freeze, Fritz's forearms got redder. Eugene's hair got bushier. Monk's sweatband got lost. Shoe rubber screeched as thugs raced and stalled, reached and stomped, roared and scrambled after the ball. Uffff. Bam. Never a swish. No first stringer shot the ball. They froze it. From me, too, their substitute teammate.

I tried once more when a General came near me. "I just wondered if you'd pass me the ball, is all."

Eugene said, "I'd rather let the air out of it," from his station at X.

"Nuts to you," shouted Fritz, passing to spot Y.

"You are heartless," I said from Z. I cut and ran my pattern.

Wheeeet. Coach quit pacing the center line. He waved his cap. He called, "Boys, what kind of stuff is that? Hagen's part of your pattern. How come you don't throw her the ball?"

Almost every General answered at once, even the second-string foulers: "Because she's on a different team—the Generalettes, *ettes*, *ettes*."

"Not for long," I thought I heard Rinehart say from the sidelines.

Chapter 7

First thing I did in homeroom Monday was measure my hands with Randy's ruler. The whole weekend I'd been squeezing a tennis ball, the way Rinehart showed me. Trying to make my hands wide as a General's. No telling when Coach O'Hara might need me to substitute, according to Rinehart, because I have more stamina than Eugene, more leadership than Fritz, more push than Ben, and more smarts than DumDum. Rinehart claimed his log could prove all that. He promised.

"Dream on," I said. "Coach won't even ask me to scrimmage with them again. Not after my shooting record—"

Zero for Zero

But anyway, I squeezed.

After I measured my hands, I stretched on tiptoe and saluted the flag. I jogged to the pencil sharpener. I turned the handle an extra long time to loosen my right wrist. I hook-shot some ancient homework into the trash basket.

"Attention, attention for Monday morning bulletins," came F. Parnell Manfred's voice over the intercom. "Our Generals' next battle pits them against the Fairfax Wolfmen this coming Friday night at eight o'clock. Good luck, boys."

I settled back in my desk to hear our own battle announced for the afternoon.

Manfred continued. "Future Cosmetologists of America meet today in Room 327. . . . Our home economics department will be selling fudge at noon to send little Miss Rae Ann Tupper to the Pillsbury Bake-Off finals. . . ."

Say, when will Manfred mention us? Our game counts more than fooling around with stoves. Maybe he's saving the best for last.

"In closing, I want to mention the girls' basketball game this afternoon, and I'm honored to confirm the rumor that yes, Miss Ruby Jean Twilly has been crowned Majorette of the Year, third year in succession. Her trophy will be retired to a prominent place in my office. We will both be interviewed today for the *Herald* by reporter Ronald Mergler, Jr."

Another ette, another photograph! Manfred loves to get his picture taken. He'll be on the *Herald* sports page tomorrow morning. And where will the Generalettes be? No one cares we're playing Swanson except my teammates and Rinehart. Thanks for the big buildup, Manfred.

I wondered about my team on the way to first period. Which five of us would be first stringers? E.J. and I had man-to-manned the other kids right off Lee's court, so I knew we'd be chosen for the 3:00 tip-off. But who else? I asked Rinehart in English class, but he couldn't answer while he wrote in his log like a fiend. I spent the whole period listing different lineups. E.J. would start at center, for sure. Me at forward. Millie the other forward? Or JoJo? And who for guards?

"Rinehart. Predict our team," I whispered.

"Evelyn Butor's choices? Impossible to second-guess the insane." He closed that subject.

Until we headed for chorus. Then I said, "E.J.'s our natural center. She's tall enough for rebounding, strong enough for blocking shots. She'll neutralize the other center anywhere on court."

Rinehart answered, "I'm more concerned about another kind of court. And my evidence here." He patted his log. His mind had clearly wandered from basketball. He offered no advice. He didn't give me his game plan the way he had last year. He was walking the halls in a dream. But I knew when the crunch came that afternoon, Rinehart would be rooting from Lee's bleachers.

Who else? Who else would watch us manhandle the Admiralettes? Not cheerleaders. None of them charged the stairs today, screaming for my autograph. And not majorettes. They never seemed to have pep left over for us girls. "We need rallies, too, you know," I muttered to Rinehart. "Sing me a fight song! Throw confetti in my hair!"

Later, trudging alone to science, I listened for one faraway cheer, but all I heard was the late bell to my final exam. Some pep rally.

Well, at least I could pass my exam. Rinehart had seen to that. Saturday when he phoned, he said, "You must boost your science average in case your grades come under examination in court."

He meant *on* court, I suppose.

"Irrelevant questions might be asked by your adversaries on the stand."

He meant Swanson's fans in the bleachers, I suppose.

"So here's what you should do. In any given true-or-false test, seventy-five percent of the sentences will be true," Rinehart explained. "Teachers find it difficult to write false statements about subjects they love. On your exam, if you print *true* in every blank, you will get at least seventy-five percent correct. In other words, C."

"Gimme a C." I cheered Rinehart's scheme.

For the first half hour of the exam, I pretended to ponder those true-false questions. Only after much pen sucking did I carefully print *true* one hundred times. Then I hurried to lunch and ate my noodles. Then math, history, study hall. No sense cutting. Snow covered our suicide field, so I couldn't work out. I warmed up for the big game with isometric exercises at my desk. I psyched myself with pepper talk: Attawaytogo, Hagen. You may be a shortie but you sure can holler and foul shoot and—and get frozen out. In the back of my mind I listened once more for Lurleen Dewey, for one stray rebel cheer filling Lee High.

Give me an H
Give me an A
Give me a GEN
HAGEN HAGEN
Yea! Yea! Yea!

All kinds of other names filled my ears instead, voices from down the hall at the gym door. “Phyllis.” “Charlotte.” “Aileen.” Our team must be gathering already. I wanted to be with them. I couldn’t wait for the final bell. I bolted from study hall. In six, eight strides I stood outside the gym, caught in a traffic jam of Generalettes.

They called out their own names. “Mildred.” “Anne.” “Aileen.” “JoAnne.” They added, “First string” or “Substitute” or “No fair” or “Who cares?” Rinehart’s voice rose about the others. “I care,” he said in the growing crowd with all eyes pinned to the door of Lee gym. All eyes read a paper nailed up high. From my trap in the crowd, I couldn’t read it.

“Excuse me,” I told my teammates. “Excuse—”

A typed lineup for the game hung directly over my head.

OFFICIAL GENERALETTES VARSITY TEAM

Evelyn Butor, Coach

Center: Aileen Dickerson
Forward: Joan Stern
Forward: Phyllis Badger
Guard: Mildred Murphy
Guard: Natalia Pysor

Substitutes: The Miller twins, Anne Bumstead, Charlotte Cardenez, Pauletta Puttsky, JoAnne Rice, and Eleanor Johnston

That team didn’t include my name! Unless—unless under a nail? Or down in a footnote? Reach that paper. Pull it off. Check the other side for *Hagen* or

Zan or *Suzanne* or—"Rinehart, my dumb name's not here."

"Doesn't surprise me," he said

"I'm benched for the season forever." I balled up the paper.

Rinehart never looked up from his log. "My experiment simply backfired," he said coolly. "I suppose we made Butor mad. So much for Plan A. We'll jump directly to Plan Z. Let's go."

I cut through my ex-teammates onto the basketball court for Rinehart's next scheme.

"Not this court," Rinehart called out. He waved his log. "My kind of court. A court of law."

Chapter 8

SCIENTIFICA RINEHARTICULUM
Daily Log of Arthur Rinehart,
Volume VIII, p. 215.

January 16, 9:37 P.M.

My experiments and observations proceeded perfectly until earlier today, when *rufus gigantus dodo* dismissed Zan from her basketball team. My best friend cried; and I noticed a certain clear fluid spilling from my own eyes. Fortunately I remembered that scientists must never show emotion.

Mrs. Butor's craven behavior means that my study of Zan's progress in athletics will remain incomplete and thus useless as a project for next year's fair. Unless, of course, I win our case in court.* If that happens, she would compete in the season's games as a General, and I would be able to collect data under ideal circumstances.

I shall record here several vital incidents precisely as they happened today.

*Actually, law is very scientific. From my research, the courtroom seems much like a laboratory: calm, orderly, businesslike. Except I'll be examining people, not snakes or tarantulas.

From 3:00 until 3:45 P.M., I explained Plan Z once again to Zan as we watched the Admiralettes pulverize her ex-team. (Final score: 54–18, Swanson.) She left the game early, before she fully believed that my plan to take her case to court would succeed. She wanted me to ask her ex-coach one more time in hopes that she would be allowed back on the team—if only as a bench warmer. I promised to try.

At 4:14 P.M. I accosted Mrs. Butor in the Lee parking lot. She seemed cheerful despite her team's humiliation. She greeted me with a slap I felt through my overcoat. She returned my numerous compliments. She asked why I was wearing Swanson's color—my maroon tie. (I deduce she finally made the color connection by noticing opposing players' uniforms.) I opened the door of her car to help her in. Before she could close it, I inquired if Zan might return to the Generalettes in any capacity. Her answer: "Never. Not even as water boy."

I asked why, but she was less specific. She ranted. I managed to take down the words *uncoachable*, *uncooperative*, *undisciplined*, and *uncouth example of young womanhood*. Since I had my briefcase open already, I showed her "certain legal papers" I plan to file tomorrow. I suggested that she would certainly be called into court as a witness. I believed this ploy might scare her, but instead she asked what I thought she should wear on the stand. Then she slammed her car door on my scarf and pulled away, nearly dragging me across Glebe Road.

See you in court, cretin *gigantus.*

To continue: Promptly at 4:30 P.M., I entered Principal Manfred's outer office for a conference regarding my suit against his school. His secretary made me wait on a bench like some truant, before she finally assured me (at 4:45) that her "boss" would be busy "for good." As I left I told her, "He certainly will be busy—on the witness stand. I'll see him there!"

My time in Manfred's outer office was not wasted. Through his half-open door, I discovered the presence of Ronald Mergler, Jr., of the *Herald*, whose camera flashed a dozen times even before Ruby Jean Twilly breezed in with her trophy. I confronted Mr. Mergler in the main hall at 5:00 P.M. I didn't need to explain who I was. He remembered taking my picture with last year's winning science project. He seemed most interested in my plan to sue Zan onto the Generals. He agreed to meet me in county court tomorrow at 10:00 A.M. to cover a "fast-breaking story." (His pun.) I plan to skip biology and chorus for this more important event.

January 16, 10:31 P.M.

Zan just phoned. She can't sleep. She wanted to know what Mrs. Butor said about returning to the team. After I read the answer, I promised Zan she will play basketball this season, over various dead bodies. "The scientific truth is, you could make any boys' team in Virginia if ability alone counted," I said to buck her up. I also promised that I'd ask Coach O'Hara "nicely" if she can play on his team—before I file for an injunction. She hung up so I wouldn't promise more.

January 17, 8:30 A.M.

For Zan's sake I visited Coach O'Hara early this morning at his house. I arrived at 7:00 and found him eating breakfast. I returned the books he lent me after Friday's scrimmage. We chatted about the full-court press. I described a semi-break offense I'd learned about in *Pro Basketball Weekly.* He drew a new get-tough defense on a paper napkin and suggested I give it to Hagen for her team. He had heard of their opening loss. What follows is a precise transcript of the rest of our conversation.

"Mr. O'Hara. Zan's team. Her plays. That's what I've come to see you about."

"How may I help you? With her natural talent—with her willingness to push herself—you shouldn't need help. She's a coach's dream."

"Not Mrs. Butor's. She refuses to let Zan play on her team."

Before I could turn my log to Butor's words, Coach said, "Foolish woman." He laid down his fork.

"Zan now hopes—we both hope—you will recruit her for your Generals."

There. I'd said it!

Just as nicely, Coach O'Hara answered, "I can't do that, Arthur." He drank his milk. Then he spoke slowly, as if figuring out his ideas for the first time. "It's not my decision alone. As principal, Mr. Manfred would have to agree on such a radical departure from policy. Knowing him, I believe he'd disagree. Further—the school board here in Arlington is bound to back him up." He munched his toast. "My team's in trouble already. We've blown our first three games. Manfred's furious."

He unfolded another napkin and wrote

1. Manfred
2. School board
3. Losing season so far

He handed me this list. He hadn't written "Hagen can't shoot" or "Hagen can't guard," so I said, "Mr. O'Hara, Zan could help your team win. She's the best second-effort player in Lee High. I've scouted them all. For my study here." I opened my log to pages of Zan's progress. "She's a ten-way marvel: faking, passing, playmaking—"

Coach O'Hara stood up to put on his jacket. He said, "Arthur, I haven't time to spell out the reasons Manfred would use to keep Hagen from joining the Generals. I'm sure a smart boy like you can imagine—"

"Zanner deserves to play for the best coach. That's what counts." I shut my log. "And you need her." When I was safely out the door and alone, I shouted, "See you in court."

January 17, 1:00 P.M.

Acting in my capacity as Zan's best friend and paralawyer, I filed, two and a half hours ago, for an injunction to keep the Generals from playing. A bona fide lawyer, E.J.'s father, stood at my side just to keep everything legal. He handled certain technical details that only a member of the Virginia Bar can perform. I will pay his fee out of my *Science Newsletter* fund.

Ronald Mergler, Jr., snapped pictures of the surprised county clerks. Judge Titus Swain rushed from his chambers to discover why the entire staff was in a panic. Mr. Mergler says his photo of Swain will be perfect on the *Herald*'s front page, along with a story under the headlines: LOCAL COED DEMANDS RIGHT TO BE A GENERAL.

After we left the courthouse, Mr. Mergler and I sat together in his car until 12:30 P.M. I showed him pages I'd photocopied from *Statutes of the State of Virginia.* I let him copy petitions, sworn statements, and data from my log. He emptied my briefcase of all the evidence (even test tubes) I plan to use in court. When he left me off at school, he said, "You have a forceful case here. For a scientist you make an excellent advocate." He gave me his home phone number. "Call me. I'll look up some information that will help you deal with the Generals' team doctor. Surely he'll be used as an expert witness. Also I'd like to read your final brief before the hearing begins."

I asked when he thought that might be.

"Judging from my past experience on the courthouse beat, I'd guess right away. The injunction will go in force immediately. That orders the Generals team to cease playing their season games until they show cause—give a reason—for keeping Zan Hagen off their squad. They must come to court before they can play ball again. Manfred won't want the boys to miss this weekend's games against—"

Mr. Mergler pulled a schedule from his wallet, but

I filled in the teams from memory: "Wolfmen and Warriors. Those would be Zan's first appearances as a General if we win our case."

"See you in court. And Zan on court!" Mr. Mergler said instead of good-bye.

January 17, Near midnight

During study hall, I took time out from writing questions (for witnesses) to practice with Zanner on her foul shooting. We cleared one end of the snowbound YMCA court. Science has no words for her determination. She's hitting 78 percent in mittens. She does not seem to fear her possible future with the unfriendly Generals. "Monk will pass to me and maybe Ben will if I curl my dumb eyelashes. Or help him unglue his feet from the boards." I quote her precisely. Soon the *Herald* will be quoting her testimony, if only she doesn't "freeze" on the witness stand.

Now I must iron my blue suit and type my opening statement.

January 18, Noon

I am writing with one hand and eating carbohydrates with the other. I'll need maximum energy by 2:30 P.M. for *Suzanne Hagen* v. *Robert E. Lee High School.* No one else in this cafeteria seems to be eating. They're all blabbering about the "trial." (A hearing is not a trial.) Mr. Mergler's three-column story in this morning's *Herald* has caused more racket than a pep rally. Randy Boyle stopped me and my alter ego on our way to English. He threatened me. He shouted an oath at Zan. Then and there I vowed not to become emotionally involved. A scientist must hold himself aloof. I allowed Zan to say the last word to him: "See you on court, teammate."

Chapter 9

"Oyez. Oyez. All rise for the judge. Thank you. Be seated."

Judge Titus Swain came into the crowded courtroom. He took his chair above us.

"Check that black robe he's wearing. Like in a movie," I whispered to my lawyer.

Rinehart whispered back. "I hope you notice I ironed my own best clothes." He dusted his lapels. "These little details will help our case." He wore a navy-blue suit with a gray shirt and tie—Generals' colors. He schemed to win them over from the first.

Just about everyone we knew had shown up in court. The front rows were stuffed with witnesses like Manfred and Coach O'Hara and Dr. Ableson, the Generals' team doctor. Next to them sat Generalettes, cheerleaders, and majorettes—our worst enemies. Then came Mrs. Butor, right where the bench sagged. Near her—well, not too near—lurked Joe Donn Joiner, captain of the Richmond Redskins basketball team. I recognized him right away because I'd seen him in games. The whole bench behind Joe Donn was taken up by Generals, who wore letter sweaters and scowls.

Those rows looked eager to testify me into oblivion!

On both sides of the aisles, parents waited for the hearing to begin. I tried to find my mother—there—

up in the gallery. I sort of half waved to her from our table in front of the judge. Mom was sitting with E.J. and Ronald Mergler, Jr.

Rinehart and I squirmed in our seats at the plaintiff's table. He shined up his cuff links, ready to present my case. I wanted to duck behind his stack of evidence and disappear. I could see Eugene Matello clenching his fist. I could hear Randy muttering, "Wait'll I give my testimony." My palms sweated. I'm doomed, I thought.

Finally Judge Swain banged his gavel. He said, "These are the proceedings of an informal inquiry into the alleged discrimination against female athletes at Robert E. Lee Junior-Senior High School, conducted in the Arlington County Courthouse this eighteenth day of January." He swung his gavel in my direction. *"Suzanne Hagen* versus *Robert E. Lee High School.* Who is representing the team?"

"I am, Judge Swain." A serious-looking man stood at the table across from ours. "I am counsel for the Arlington County Schools."

"And who is representing the girl, Suzanne Hagen?"

Rinehart gave a quick bow. "I am, Your Honor."

Judge Swain peered down from his platform. "Highly irregular," he said and pursed his lips. "Why does Miss Hagen not retain the services of a person admitted to the Virginia State Bar?"

In answer, Rinehart read from his log. He must have known the judge would challenge his right to speak for me in court because his answer went on and on. He kept calling himself a "para-lawyer." He defined the difference between a "trial" and an "ordinary, casual hearing." He spoke of the "quasi-legal" reasons for anyone to be present in the courtroom at all. He said if the hearing had been held in Lee auditorium, as he had requested, I wouldn't have needed even a para-lawyer. I could have represented myself. He ended by saying, "In short, Your Honor, at a *gathering* such as this where there are no crooks and no crimes except that of discrimination—"

"Discrimination has yet to be established," interrupted the school's counsel.

"I apologize for that error," Rinehart told the counsel and smiled. He paused to sip from a handy paper cup. I could smell Gatorade. He must be thirsting for battle, but he said meekly, "I am Arthur Rinehart, resident of Virginia, a student at Lee High, and a dedicated scholar of the law."

For the past two weeks, I happened to know.

He continued in his begging voice. "Here in this hostile atmosphere, where I am the only friend Miss Hagen has, well, I am hoping—we are both hoping you will allow me to speak for this poor girl."

Judge Swain seemed moved by Rinehart's beg. Or confused by his mumbo jumbo. He looked over at the school's counsel for help. So did Rinehart. Rinehart flashed his dazed, dopey expression, the one he springs on someone he wants to fake out.

Counsel must have figured he could beat Rinehart easily. He said, "I have no objections to this young man's representing Miss Hagen."

"And you, Miss Hagen. Are you positive you wish this young man to state your case? Has he knowledge of the issues?"

"He reads a lot" is all I managed to testify.

Judge Swain looked at the wall clock and shook his head. He said, "We are all anxious to settle this matter so that the basketball season may proceed smoothly. You are correct, Mr. Rinehart. This is indeed an informal questioning into the problems Miss Hagen has raised, even though we will be using certain court formalities. I accept you as advocate."

He sat back to gaze at me and my pal while the clerk announced, "In the matter of *Hagen* versus *Lee High School.* Counsel for the school, you may open your case."

The counsel rose stiffly from his table. He advanced toward me with slow steps. He held up his arm. He pointed a finger and said, "You, my dear, are causing the school considerable trouble, time, and monies that might be spent on important projects." He dropped his arm in disgust. "I intend to make short work of this asinine matter."

With that, Counsel settled down to his opening statement. Rinehart took notes madly on a long yellow tablet. I bit my fingernails, feeling guilty already.

"In the course of this hearing, I will present experts who will refute Miss Hagen's claim to a place on the Generals' roster. Your Honor, ladies and gentlemen, you will hear testimony to support the school's position that one—"

Counsel held up his pointing finger.

"One, there are proper teams for Miss Hagen to join—female teams that have the blessing of tradition. And two—"

Counsel held up another finger. Together, the fingers made a victory V.

"Two, Miss Hagen is not suited, by reason of her

femaleness, to become a Lee General." Counsel waved the V at me. "Furthermore, we are confident that this case will set a precedent for other school districts in our great state. When the Right Honorable Titus Swain rules in our favor, persons of the female sex will stay on their own designated teams throughout Virginia, rather than trouble mankind with injunctions and suits and—and whatnot."

Without another glance at me, Counsel strode back to his seat. I hung my head, feeling guiltier. Rinehart sat without a word, without an objection. He arranged a row of pencils on our table. When he stood up to make his opening statement, he was as calm as if he were looking into his microscope.

"Your Honor and fellow rooters for the Robert E. Lee Generals. I'm certain that you are as impressed as I am by Counsel's—hmmmmm—well-chosen words." He smiled at Counsel. "I am equally certain that you will be interested in my evidence that Zan Hagen is being unfairly and illegally barred from the Generals team, a team that would benefit from her capable help as it attempts to reach a post-season tournament."

"Sumkinda stupid help she'd be in the *Herald* finals," Randy said aloud.

"Silence in this court," called the clerk.

I didn't think Rinehart heard Randy until he tossed aside his legal pad and turned toward the judge. He asked, "Does Zan Hagen look stupid, Your Honor? Does she look like a troublemaker? I want you to change places with her, sir. I want you to hear what she hears. Feel what she feels. As the counsel presents his case against girls—against Zan—I want you to step into Zan's shoes."

My feet burned when Rinehart said that.

"Your Honor, once you are standing in those Keds, you will feel what it's like to be sneered at, to be rejected, to be 'only' a girl, as Zan's tormentors would say. A girl who wants only the same rights as our county gives to boys." Rinehart looked straight at the judge, said "Thank you, sir," and sat down.

Judge Swain said, "Call the first witness for Lee."

"Dr. Ableson, please take the stand."

The doctor left his front-row seat in a hurry. He seemed raring to score points for the Generals. He settled himself in the witness chair, folded his hands on his stomach, and answered, "I am Leon Ableson, team physician for the Lee Generals. I have held that position for the past twenty years. In those two decades, the teams have won many championships, all of them without the benefit of young ladies!"

Counsel smiled at his witness and said, "Tell us in your own words, Doctor, why you believe that females should not be accepted on *your* teams of the future."

"Gladly." The doctor smiled back. "To begin with, there are medical reasons. Ladies—girls are not built the same as boys. Girls are softer, more tender and delicate; boys are tough—stronger, faster, quicker. Girls would sustain massive injuries if they were permitted to engage in athletics on the same teams with boys. That would mean girls would have to play *against* boys as well as *with* them." He declared *against* as if he'd just thought of it for the first time. He added, "That would mean girls would get banged around pretty badly. And that wouldn't be a good situation, would it?"

A stir ran through the court. Mothers gasped. Fathers shifted their feet. In the confusion, Rinehart whispered, "That doctor is scoring with the judge. Swain's face—he's hurting for you already, Zanner."

"Silence!"

Counsel knew his case was going well. He strutted toward the witness, saying, "Dr. Ableson, what other conclusions have you reached in regard to females playing against boys?"

"Girls would become unfeminine. They would grow muscular and unattractive. Lumpy, perhaps. Oh my, my. I do not approve of young ladies as Generals on any grounds whatsoever." The doctor looked at me again.

"Thank you, Doctor." Counsel seemed satisfied as he sat back down.

"Mr. Rinehart, you may cross-examine," said Judge Swain from far away. He seemed satisfied, too. I felt sure he would rule against me then and there unless—unless Rinehart could somehow make the doctor look like a quack. Then no one would believe his "expert" testimony. "Go get 'em," I whispered to my pal.

Rinehart gathered his notes. He approached the witness stand. He rested his left hand against the bar and turned sideways so he could see both doctor and judge. He opened his cross-examination with "Now, Doctor, you say you have been the one and only team physician for two decades?"

ABLESON: Yes, I have been.

RINEHART: And you have had occasion to treat injured Generals over those many years?

ABLESON: Yes, I have.

RINEHART: Did you, for example, treat Paul (Beanball) Muggins some time ago?

ABLESON: I did.

RINEHART: Would you mind my asking how he is now?

ABLESON: Poor boy, he is still on crutches.

RINEHART: Were you not the doctor in the end zone when R.C. (Cola) Jackson fell against the goalpost?

ABLESON: I was.

RINEHART: I haven't heard about Mr. Jackson lately. Could you bring me up to date?

ABLESON: Cola is at home, in a wheelchair, I believe. I am no longer his physician.

RINEHART: But you are still the attending physician for "Slamming" Sam Matthews, are you not?

ABLESON: No, I am not.

RINEHART: May I ask why?

ABLESON: He is dead!

Another stir ran through the court, but Rinehart didn't wait for the clerk to call "Silence." He pressed on with more questions while the doctor folded and unfolded his hands.

RINEHART: Perhaps I should change the subject from your, uh, failures as a physician to your achievements. I understand you are also team doctor for the Generalettes. Would you be kind enough to describe your duties to the court?

ABLESON: Duties? I have only one duty. I examine these girls once each year to make sure they are healthy enough to indulge in their own sports: field hockey, softball, volleyball, and, er, basketball.

RINEHART: And over the years you have found . . . ?

ABLESON: Nothing special. Girls of usual heights, weights. All in apparent good health. Just your typical, average girls.

RINEHART: I see. And you've never had occasion to examine these same girls after they compete in any of these sports you name?

ABLESON: No.

RINEHART: But Dr. Ableson, might not these girls need your services during and after games? If, as you have testified, girls are soft, tender, delicate, would they not need your skilled help in case of injury?

ABLESON: No injury has ever been brought to my attention. No girl has sought me out. I assume no one has ever been hurt.

RINEHART: Don't you find that odd, sir, that year after year in competition, these delicate girls come through their sports wars without disaster?

ABLESON: Ahem, ahem. I seem to recall—yes, there was one injury. To Miss Hagen. She stopped me last autumn sometime. She showed me a swollen finger.

RINEHART: Tell us, Doctor, how do you treat a General's swollen finger? Randy Boyle's, for instance?

ABLESON: Oh, with pain-killers, whirlpool baths, and whatnot.

RINEHART: And how did you treat Miss Hagen's

badly mangled finger that November day, if you don't mind my asking?

ABLESON: Well, I was in a hurry at the time and it didn't seem so serious, so I told her to go home and put a hot compress on it.

Rinehart eyed Ableson a long time. Then he said, "Thank you, Doctor. No further questions. Please step down."

When Rinehart came back to our table, I said, "Attaboy, lawyer." I poured two cups of Gatorade. I lifted mine for a toast to his victory over the school's first witness. Rinehart whispered, "One down, worse to come." He mopped his brow with a gray handkerchief while he watched a parade of Generals take the stand.

First DumDum Cadden. He must have stuck his gum under the bench, because he never popped it once in his whole testimony. He answered most questions with "Nope" or "Yep." Nope, he wouldn't play on the same team with a girl freak. Yep, he planned to grow a mustache for the *Herald* Tournament and, hahahaha, no girl could do that. Nope, no girl could learn the Generals' "hard" plays, especially page 1 to the end of the playbook. "She's too dumb," he said.

"Objection, Your Honor," called Rinehart.

"Objection sustained. The witness must not indulge in name-calling," Judge Swain cautioned DumDum over laughter from the audience. But Counsel was finished with DumDum anyway. He said, "Your witness," to Rinehart and sat down.

"I do not wish to cross-examine Mr. Walter Cadden," Rinehart answered from our table.

"Call the next witness."

Eugene Matello testified that he'd rot first before he'd play with a girl on *any* team, even the New York Knicks. What's more, he wouldn't undress in the same locker room with *any* girl, even if she did have stamina like Coach said.

Rinehart didn't object and he didn't cross-examine.

Ben Brown testified that he'd never let a lady become a General, especially a lady who was making a fuss in court. "Ladies are supposed to be pretty and weak," he declared firmly, not "tricky" and "pushy." He wouldn't let his girlfriend, DeeDee Tupper, try out for sports, even girls' sports, because she might get fat legs like the doc said.

Rinehart had no questions about legs or anything.

Fritz Slappy said that he agreed with everything Boyle would testify next. "Ditto, ditto, ditto," he called to Randy.

Rinehart sat without a question for Fritz. I hid my eyes, feeling guiltier and guiltier. I listened to Randy rattle off his answers.

"Basketball's a contact sport . . . lots of knocks and bangs . . . lots of body, er, er, contact. . . . I don't want to crash against a girl, at least not on the basketball court. . . . Hahaha. . . . Hagen's a jock but she never earned a letter sweater like me and my team. . . . Anyway, she's too short to be a General. . . . Girls are midgets. . . . I won't play with her. . . . Never! I'll cut down the nets first. Never!"

"Your witness," Counsel called over a Randy Boyle *never.*

Rinehart said, "I waive my right to cross-examine Mr. Boyle."

"Why?" I whispered. I was beginning to feel abandoned by my lawyer. I reached over to touch him, just to make sure he was really there. He scribbled himself notes on a legal pad as Monk Cunningham sat down in the witness chair.

"State your name."

"John Cunningham. Kids call me 'Monk' because I cross myself before I go to the foul line. Also because I wear this." He pulled his St. Christopher medal from under his shirt.

"Tell us, Mr. Cunningham, how you feel about having a female on your team," Counsel said.

"I'd rather not."

"Witness will answer the question," Judge Swain cautioned.

"I mean I'd rather not have girls on the basketball team."

"Tell us why, Mr. Cunningham." Counsel smiled at his witness, trying to draw out the answers he wanted to hear.

Monk spun his medal on its chain. He thought awhile before he said quietly, "I suppose I've never figured out why."

"Figure out *now.*" Counsel was growing impatient. So were the Generals. They stretched around and whispered together, waiting for their teammate to drive another nail in my coffin.

Monk surprised them. He said, "It's not that I don't like girls. I do. I wouldn't mind them beside me in the center-jump circle. I bet some of them could take their knocks like the rest of us. I wouldn't even mind if they came into our locker room. I mean, how else could they hear Coach O'Hara's pep talk at the half? I guess they'd be okay in our steam bath, too. What harm could they do?"

Counsel gave Monk a cold nod. "*I* am asking the questions, not *you*, my boy. Now, you stated that you would rather not have females play on the Generals basketball team. This court is wondering exactly why you'd rather not."

"I suppose"—Monk began in an almost whisper—"I suppose it's because I want our team to win. I want to beat the other guys in our league. Admirals, Wolfmen, Eagles, all of them. Even though we've lost three straight, I'm praying us Generals will be there in the *Herald* Tournament this spring."

That's what I'm hoping, with me on the team, I almost called to Monk. But Counsel butted in. He said, "In other words, Mr. Cunningham, you believe that the Generals could not be winners with females holding down any position on your roster?"

Even substitutes? I almost called. Even if I warmed the bench and never played except when we got fifty points ahead? I wanted to ask old Monk that question and some others, but he was busy saying, "I feel we would lose with girls on the team."

"Thank you. Your witness, Mr. Rinehart."

I was sure that Rinehart wouldn't cross-examine Monk. After all, he'd already let the other Generals slip off the stand without a question. He sat beside me now, moving nothing but his pen. He made long dashes after certain words: *freak*, *retard*, *girl*. He drew a question mark next to *lose*. Just when I decided Rinehart would start doodling commas, he confronted the witness with:

"Monk, I gather from your testimony that you wouldn't mind playing on the same team with a girl as long as your team wins."

Monk's eyes flew wide open. "Did I say that?" He rubbed his medal against his cheek as he thought. "Well, yes, you could dope it out that way, couldn't you?"

His teammates answered by shuffling their feet. Randy hissed, "Traitor."

Rinehart pressed on with his next questions. "Monk, you seem to speak from experience. Have you ever played basketball with a girl on your team?"

"No!" He nodded at the Generals. They whistled their approval.

"Not even in a practice session?"

"Well, yes, once. Last Friday."

Rinehart said, "Ah, as recently as that. Which girl played on your side that day? If you see her in court, point her out to the judge." Rinehart moved toward his witness with sure steps.

Monk gave his medal a nervous flick. He pointed to me. I tried to grin, but my mouth froze at the icy stares coming from all directions.

"Now, Monk, everyone here knows that basketball practices are run at a furious pace. Each player is busy with his own moves. You may not have been able to observe Zan carefully."

"But I—"

"Monk, you will certainly be forgiven if you cannot comment on Zan's part in practice."

"Forgiven? But I did watch her. We played on the same team, remember. We were supposed to help each other. Coach kept telling us. I tried to help her."

"Will you please describe Zan in action," Rinehart said, practically head to head with his witness.

Monk squared his shoulders. He slowly told the court, "She—Zan—she ran—she jumped. She hung in there." He looked at me. "She outplayed her guards. She had all kinds of moves." He looked at his teammates. "She learned the freeze pattern; boy, did she learn. She ran to her spots. She's agile. She's a fighter. She took her licks and didn't complain." He looked at Judge Swain. "Hagen psyched out Brown in the jump circle and he complained. Her timing is super. She—" Monk paused to think what else.

Rinehart asked, "And her style of play? Is it freaky? Retarded?"

Monk answered, "No." He looked at Counsel.

"And you didn't find her too short to be effective?"

"No, not for a guard. I'm a guard because I'm shorter than the other guys," Monk admitted, looking at his own feet. "And there's a guy in the NBA who plays around second string—he's only five feet six. Playing's about attitude!"

"Thank you, Monk. You've been most helpful." Rinehart started toward our desk smiling and ready to attack a ton of witnesses. But before he could sit down, Counsel called across the court, "I would like to redirect one question to Mr. Cunningham, if I may."

"Certainly," Judge Swain said.

Looking directly at me, Counsel asked, "Mr. Cunningham, did Miss Hagen make any baskets during that eventful practice session you've described so sensitively?"

"Huh?"

"Did she score?"

"Well, no."

"Thank you. You've answered *the* important question."

Chapter 10

Poor Rinehart! He still hadn't sat down. He seemed to be in shock. His eyes watered behind his glasses. His lips formed the silent word *score*. He held his log in one hand as if he planned a hook shot of his own—at the trash basket. He moved sideways to our table, careful to stay away from the next witness.

"I am Joe Donn Joiner, captain of the Richmond School basketball team." Joe Donn hadn't even noticed Rinehart.

Counsel said, "Mr. Joiner, the court thanks you for hurrying from southern Virginia to answer just two small questions." Counsel waited for everyone's attention. "Would you and your Redskins play against the Generals in, say, the *Herald* Tournament if Suzanne Hagen were on their team?"

"No man, we wouldn't."

"Would you play against *any* basketball team on which there were female members?"

"No! No way! Nohow! Nowhere!"

"Your witness, Mr. Rinehart."

Rinehart didn't need to stand up to cross-examine Joe Donn. He was still up, if you could call it that. He sagged against our table, head hung low. Even his gray tie had gone limp. He moved his lips, but this time they didn't form *score*. Instead he said to the judge, "Your Honor, we request a recess."

Judge Swain tapped his gavel lightly. He called,

"Court is adjourned until seven o'clock tonight." He gathered his robe around himself and hurried from the room.

Poor Rinehart! He wouldn't touch the dinner Mom had packed us in a picnic basket. I tried to cheer him with carrot sticks and jokes about Joe Donn's swell personality. I tried to laugh off my zero scrimmage with the Generals. "I should've shot my shoe for two," I said, offering Rinehart our entire deviled egg supply.

"If you'd only stolen the ball and scored, Zan. Next time you will, don't worry." He said that grimly. Then he didn't say anything. He fell to work on his notes. He wrote questions for Mrs. Butor, Counsel's next witness after the recess. He traced his pencil over a paragraph he hoped to read aloud to F. Parnell Manfred. While I polished off every cupcake, he drew exclamation points beside Coach O'Hara's name. "O'Hara's the crucial witness," Rinehart muttered. "My case depends on how he testifies—and on whether you hold up under Counsel's cross-examination, Zan." He ate a crumb.

"How come you didn't cross-examine DumDum or Eugene or Ben or Fritz or Randy?"

"Because they didn't hurt our case one bit. Juries—judges tend to ignore testimony from such mean, biased witnesses. It says right here." He patted a thick book on top of his stack. I read it until we trooped back to our table in court.

As soon as we sat down again, Rinehart asked me in a whisper, "What happens when one team refuses to play another? Like say the Redskins decide not to play a scheduled game. They stay home in Richmond that night. Or walk off your court at the half."

"They forfeit. Once last year the Wolfettes didn't want to come to our gym during an ice storm. Us Generalettes were dressed and ready to play. The Wolfettes had to forfeit." That was all I could whisper before Judge Swain swished through the green padded doors. Joe Donn Joiner already waited in the witness chair.

"Are you prepared to cross-examine Counsel's witness now, Mr. Rinehart?" The judge said *prepared* loud.

"I am, Your Honor." Rinehart carried his dictionary with him.

"Proceed."

Rinehart greeted Joe Donn with a casual nod. He said, "The court thanks you again for traveling all the way from Richmond to answer two more tiny questions. However, before I ask them, I want to read you something from this dictionary I hold in my right hand." He opened to a page I couldn't see. He read in a clear voice: " 'Forfeit. To lose a game (such as tennis, hockey, basketball) by refusing to play.' Lose! Lose!"

A gasp came from the front row.

Rinehart turned away from his witness and looked at me. "And so, Joe Donn, let's suppose that Zan Hagen, by a freakish accident or by simple justice, becomes a General. Let's suppose you see her suited up in blue and gray, about to come onto the court against your Redskins. Would you then refuse to play?"

"Er, like I said before dinner. Er, like I told the other guy over there. Er, we wouldn't play ball. Me and my guys wouldn't."

"Meaning you would forfeit?" Rinehart asked his second question.

Joe Donn looked ready to part with his dinner.

"Meaning you would automatically lose? Say yes or no, Captain Joiner." Rinehart bashed his dictionary against the bar.

"Witness will answer the question." Judge Swain helped him along.

"Er. Er. Er. Yes, I guess so. Yes."

Rinehart ran his eyes along a row of Generals. He stopped at Monk. "Yes, lose. The Redskins would lose." He whirled to face his witness. "Lose even in the *Herald* Tournament."

Joe Donn covered his mouth and fled his seat. And the courtroom.

Coach Evelyn Butor replaced Joe Donn on the stand. Watching her drop her bulk into the witness chair, Rinehart wrote me a note: "I hope she doesn't fit." She fit with a few twists. Rinehart's pencil raced to keep up with her definite opinions. In the hour she spoke, he listed these main arguments:

1. Young ladies—bones more fragile. (Wrong)
2. " " —more likely to be injured. (Wrong)
3. Hormones. (She doesn't know what she's talking about.)
4. Proper teams for young ladies. (Mrs. Butor's teams!)

"Nothing new except hormones," Rinehart whispered just before Counsel turned over his witness for cross-examination.

And right then my lawyer stood up and demolished Mrs. Butor's opinions. Rinehart made statements in the form of questions, citing tests from *Athletic Journal* proving girls' bones are smaller than boys' but no more fragile. Other recent tests prove boys are bigger and stronger but girls are more flexible, with better balance. From *Coaches' Quarterly*, Rinehart read aloud a study of sports injuries—fewer for girls than for boys. He walked back and forth waving papers. One by one he picked apart Mrs. Butor's testimony until her voice grew dull saying yes.

"Yes, I suppose muscles are not basically ugly. . . . Yes, I required the girls' basketball team to bake brownies to pay for their costumes. . . . Yes, I know that boys don't go near stoves to finance their uniforms. . . . Yes, I'm quite certain about hormones. They're fluids . . . or juices . . . something that makes young ladies different from boys."

"Like pink booties?" Rinehart asked.

Even Judge Swain laughed.

Rinehart wasn't finished. He persuaded Mrs. Butor to describe the girls' locker room. When she bragged about mirrors, he read his questions about leaking showers, hingeless locker doors, and bulbless lights. He pushed her about clean towels, sauna baths, rubdown tables.

She told the court, "Young ladies don't need frills."

"We're not speaking of young ladies now. We're speaking of athletes—girls or boys." Rinehart held up a test tube of green water. "Do you recognize this, Mrs. Butor?"

She didn't.

"This is footbath solution from the girls' shower room. Did you mix that solution?"

"Yes, of course."

Rinehart swiftly reported that a well-known laboratory had analyzed the contents as dangerous. "Foot poison," he told the witness and everyone. "You might as well have used deadly nightshade. I introduce this slime in evidence. Thank you, Coach Butor. That is all."

She remained in her chair long enough to give Rinehart a withering look. Randy blurted, "I hope Arthur Rinehart drowns in that stuff." Cheerleaders chipped in *yeas*. Counsel put his head together with Manfred, plotting revenge, no doubt. I could tell our opponents weren't giving up yet.

"Half our case depends on you, Zan," Rinehart whispered.

I felt my palms itch like when I took crisis foul shots. I tried to imagine what I'd say to Counsel's questions. I looked at Rinehart for comfort. He gave his most encouraging frown.

"The other half depends on Coach O'Hara. If he testifies for their side, I'll never break him. He's got too much class." Rinehart hardly paid attention to Manfred on the stand. Instead he leaned sideways at our table to watch Coach, who hadn't returned to the front row after recess. Coach sat further back, alone by a window. Whose side would he be on when it came his turn in the witness chair? I wondered while listening to Counsel question Manfred.

"Principal Manfred, as our next-to-last witness, I'd like you to tell this court in detail your numerous reasons for wanting Suzanne to play basketball on her own team—the Femalettes, if I might call it that for the moment."

Manfred reared up and grinned at his audience, as if posing for a picture. He glanced around for reporters. His black suit shined where he slapped his knee for emphasis. "Suzanne a Femalette? Yes, yes, as long as I am principal of Robert E. Lee." After this outbreak he got down to business on details. "I'm thinking of Suzanne's *safety.* The young girl would be *bruised and banged.* She would draw many *fouls* from boys. Then there's the question of *money. Crowds* would stop coming to Generals games, and we can't afford to lose those ticket dollars. *Newspapers* would call me *crazy.* Me. F. Parnell Manfred." He saluted the balcony, where he had finally spotted Ronald Mergler, Jr.

I couldn't listen to Manfred's details any longer. I read the thickest lawbook on our table until Rinehart's cross-examination began. Once my lawyer started talking, a deep silence came over the court. Here was a student speaking up to—talking back to—his principal.

"Facts. Let us consider the facts, Mr. Manfred. You have speculated that if Zan were a General, she would be deliberately fouled by boys in games."

"Yes, I am sure she would be."

"All right. I will accept your speculation. Did you know that Hagen's foul-shooting average, as of this morning's practice, is seventy-eight percent?" Rinehart didn't give the witness a chance to answer. "Did you also know that the Generals' team foul-shooting average is sixty-three percent?" Again Rinehart plunged ahead, not waiting for answers. "Those are facts, sir. Put those facts together with your speculation, and you have Hagen scoring many points for her team, the Generals."

"Objection. Miss Suzanne is not a General."

"Sustained. I advise *you* to stay with the facts, Mr. Rinehart." Judge Swain shot my lawyer a warning eyebrow.

"Yes, Your Honor. I mean to." Rinehart's back stiffened. "Mr. Manfred, you announced earlier that Zan Hagen would always be a Femalette—uh—Generalette, as long as you are principal."

"Correct, Arthur."

Rinehart's eyes flashed behind his glasses. "Is it a fact, sir, that you are still principal of Lee High this very second?"

"Of course. What a silly question."

"Then as principal, are you aware of the following fact? Zan Hagen is not now a Generalette!" Rinehart didn't pause for an answer. "She was cut from that team by Evelyn Butor, just the day before yesterday." Rinehart's voice rose and rose. "It is a further fact that both Generals and Generalettes are beyond your control, that they are in the hands of their coaches, who make all decisions about who will play and who will not!"

"Objection. Objection. Mr. Rinehart is browbeating this witness."

Judge Swain didn't call "Sustained." He swiveled

his chair closer to Rinehart. "Can this be true? You are claiming that your client is not even a Femalette—a Generalette?"

Rinehart nodded yes.

"Is this true, Mr. Manfred?"

Astonished, Manfred waved to Mrs. Butor.

"Truth, Coach Butor?" The judge seemed just as surprised as I had been when I couldn't find my name on her typed team.

Mrs. Butor wasn't about to answer the question simply. From the front row, she recited her reasons for dumping me off the ettes, ending with "I haven't seen Mr. Manfred since last week."

"Tell me now—again," Mr. Manfred said with obvious glee.

"Suzanne's aggressive, pushy, bangy—"

The front rows clapped agreement.

Rinehart didn't object. He sat down. He poked me for good cheer. "Let her rave on," he whispered. "She's making my own final point with Manfred." On his ruled pad, Rinehart drew a large **Z** followed by small letters I couldn't see.

Judge Swain stopped Mrs. Butor with a raised hand. "You have answered my question. And more." He looked at his watch. He pointed his gavel at Rinehart. "Please conclude your cross-examination of Principal Manfred."

Rinehart tore off his top-sheet **Z**. He carried it and nothing else with him. No lawbooks, no dictionary this time. He spoke to Manfred in an approving tone. "Sir, you have joined the previous witnesses in expressing fear for Zan Hagen on the basketball court. You yourself have used such words as *safety*, *bruises*, *bangs*. You may recall words spoken earlier today: *massive injuries*, *clouts*, *knocks*, *contact*, *Smithereen City*, *bangings*, and—"

"Yes," Manfred interrupted. "We are all concerned with Miss Suzanne's health."

"Admirable, sir." Rinehart stepped closer to the witness chair. "Yet—I'm wondering—did it ever occur to you that Zan can take care of herself? You have heard her described as *smart*, *hardworking*, *a scrapper*, *tough*, *aggressive*, *a fighter*."

Manfred noisily cleared his throat. He said, "Arthur, for a young lady these are not words of praise, you understand."

Rinehart stood tall against the bar of justice. "Why aren't they, sir?"

Manfred had no answer.

"Never mind. My client expects no praise from Arlington County or its schools. She expects fair play. If it is indeed a fact that Zan Hagen is pushy and bangy, doesn't it follow that on the basketball court she will never allow herself to be trampled?" Rinehart's voice climbed to its top pitch. "Isn't it a fact that in a game, the Hagen described today would act like Randy Boyle or Fritz Slappy or Joe Donn Joiner? She would bang back!"

Manfred seemed embarrassed by the thought. He hid his eyes. He said, "I should surely hope not."

"Stuff your hopes, Mr. Manfred. Zan is no cream puff. She will come through the Generals' winning season unharmed. She's a real Zanbanger."

Chapter 11

"Zanbanger!" repeated Lurleen Dewey. "Zanbanger" went the word from row to row. Up front, Judge Swain asked Counsel, "Have you further witnesses to present?"

"One witness, Your Honor. The Generals' coach."

Rinehart didn't flinch.

"And you, Mr. Rinehart. How many witnesses will testify for the plaintiff?"

"One." Rinehart said this in a commanding voice. "Also I have a long summation."

The judge yawned. He consulted his watch. "Would you gentlemen object if we adjourn for the night? Most of this audience should be in bed already."

Rinehart objected. Counsel didn't.

"Objection overruled. Court stands adjourned until Thursday, January nineteenth, at two o'clock, when Counsel's final witness will be Coach Michael O'Hara."

Beaming triumphantly, Counsel left court, pushing his way through the crowd. He caught up with Coach O'Hara and took his arm. "You're my star attraction," he said so that reporters could hear. He beamed again with Manfred and Randy for the cameras. All three would be in the *Herald* tomorrow under a headline I could imagine: CUNNING COUNSEL CRUSHES COED'S CASE.

Rinehart and I backed into an elevator unnoticed behind our piles of books. We rode down to the first floor without even seeing Coach O'Hara in the corner until he asked me, "Is your foul-shooting average really seventy-eight percent?"

Rinehart said yes for me.

"Where is she practicing?"

"YMCA. Outside on asphalt. I shake salt on the ice. Zan shovels snow," Rinehart had time to mumble before we faced another mob in the lobby.

"Let her through," Coach said to them.

And next afternoon in court he said nothing. On the dot of two o'clock when Judge Swain called him to the stand, Coach answered, "I decline, Your Honor. I prefer not to testify." He stayed in his back-row seat.

You could have heard a swish shot in that huge room, it got so quiet. The Generals were too stunned to challenge their silent coach. Counsel looked off into space, wondering what had happened to his star. After a while he stammered, "The county—er—our varsity team—er—rests—er—its case." His eyes zeroed in on me as if to add "I'll soon get around to cross-examining you." I heard my heart beat under my dumb brown jumper, my court dress.

Rinehart leaned over to whisper, "Don't let Counsel fool you. He's not resting. He's hovering like a spider to catch us. Are you ready for my two questions? For his?"

I heard my voice crack "Yes."

"Mr. Rinehart, call your only witness." Judge

Swain watched me sway against our table. I stumbled across court and tripped on the steps to the stand.

I sat down. I listened hard to Rinehart's first question.

"Zan Hagen. Do you want to play basketball for the Generals?"

"I do," I breathed.

"You what? Tell this court, my girl," urged the judge.

"I do." I stood up to say it.

Rinehart asked his second question. "Zan Hagen. Do you believe you can help the Generals have a championship season?"

That one didn't throw me either. "I do," I called out, still standing.

"Thank you," Rinehart said as casually as if I'd just finished admiring his stuffed gerbil. "The plaintiff rests."

Rests? I slumped, that's what. Soon as I saw my pal turn away and Counsel stalk toward me, I slid down in my chair, trying to hide. He'd never let me rest.

"Suzanne." Counsel paused in front of me. He cocked his head. He seemed to doubt whether it would be worth his effort to question me.

Meanwhile I squirmed. I shoved my feet far under the chair, then out, then back. I rolled my head around on my neck. I nearly wore out my brown jumper, smoothing the skirt. Hoping to find a friend, I looked around the courtroom. I looked and looked.

Counsel broke into my search. In his kindest tone all trial, he purred, "Suzanne, I'd like to conduct an uncross-examination, for I believe you and I are on the same side, after all."

What could I say to that? Nothing.

"Suzanne, I love athletics. And you love athletics, won't you confess?"

"I confess." What else could I say?

"Then that means we both love competition, yes or no?"

"Yes, sir," I had to admit.

"Moreover, I respect the Generals. Do you respect them as well?"

"Yes, sir."

"Loving competition as we both do, we wouldn't want to see *our* Generals win their games by forfeit—I mean, do forfeits prove which team is really the champion?"

"No." I was catching on, but I had to say the truth.

"Ah! We are on the same side." Counsel offered me a drink of water. I needed it a lot. He let me swallow the whole glass before he said, "Now tell us, Suzanne, about your dunk shot."

I choked. I gasped out "I can't, sir."

"Why?"

"I don't have a dunk shot. I'm not tall enou—" I caught myself.

"That's all right, my dear. Describe to us your tip-in baskets."

I sat without a word.

"Did I ask you a question?" Counsel demanded.

"Yes, sir."

"Then why haven't you answered it?"

"I don't make many tip-ins."

"May I ask why?" When I kept my mouth shut, Counsel didn't press me. He stopped messing around with the subtle questions. He went straight for my throat. "How tall are you, Suzanne?"

"Almost as tall as Monk Cunningham, sir."

Counsel stroked his chin. "No wonder you can't dunk or stuff or tip or rebound or block shots or be of any value to a team or—"

Rinehart came to my rescue. "I object, Your Honor." Judge Swain agreed. "Stay with the questions, Counsel. You must not comment."

Counsel made a humming noise in his throat. He strode away from me. I thought he was finished until he suddenly said, "My dear, you claim you will be able to help the Generals. Help them what?" While I thought up a complete sentence, he paced along the bar. He eyed my outstretched Keds. "Help them in a game? But we have already established that you don't score points! Or perhaps you plan to help with team morale?"

I pulled in my feet and thought about that one.

Counsel didn't give me forever. "But what sort of *fellow*ship could the Generals maintain with you in their locker room? They couldn't even change into their uniforms."

"I wouldn't look," I said, practically in Counsel's ear.

He didn't listen. He shouted, "How can the team cure their aches and pains with you in their steam bath? The place would be chaos. Lee High would be the laughingstock of Virginia."

It was my turn to talk. I could tell because Counsel's mouth was closed and everyone else's hung open. Rinehart said, "Objection." The judge chipped in with "Sustained."

"I don't take it back. Yes, I could help the Generals in games. Then I'd go in my own locker room to change. I'd—"

"Thank you. That is all" was Counsel's total answer. He moved aside as I crept off the stand. He said, "Your Honor, I won't bother with a summation. Please allow Arthur Rinehart to make his final statement, if he believes he still has a case."

That seemed to be a signal for the far rows to leave. Kids charged out of court, even though a clerk and Judge Swain called for order. Pretty soon half the benches were empty, including Coach O'Hara's. I searched for him in a crowd of parents filing up the aisle. I thought I'd see him deserting my sunk ship. Instead I found him right there at our table, holding a notebook of his own.

Coach said to Rinehart, "I'd like to be your second witness if I may."

Rinehart blinked up from his frantic writing. He gave out a yell of surprise that could have been heard to Richmond. He flailed his arms, trying for Judge Swain's attention. "May it please the court. Plaintiff desires to present one more witness. One."

"Most unusual." The judge spun his gavel. "Nevertheless, I shall grant this request if you make it your last." Rap. Rap. "Call the second witness."

Coach O'Hara and Rinehart walked together toward the stand. I wish they could have seen Counsel's expression as he watched them take their places. His mouth looked like Rinehart had fed him a formaldehyde lizard.

"What is your name and occupation?"

"I am Michael O'Hara. I coach the Generals varsity

teams. Football. Basketball. Baseball. Boys' varsity."

Rinehart seemed stumped for another question. His notes were useless because he hadn't prepared to meet Coach as a friendly witness. I knew Rinehart stood there deciding what to ask now. Even with his back to me, I could see his scheming expression, his eyes scrunched up behind his slipping-off glasses.

Rinehart asked what everyone in court wanted to know. "Coach O'Hara, what finally brings you to the stand?"

Coach waited. Not because he needed attention. The rows were more silent than when he wouldn't testify for Counsel. And not because he wasn't prepared. He'd carried along his navy-blue notebook. So why was he there with his mouth shut? And then why did he turn toward Judge Swain with an apology?

"Your Honor. And you, Arthur. I'm sorry."

Counsel almost bit his pencil in half with anticipation. Maybe Coach wouldn't testify for the plaintiff after all.

"I'm sorry to say that I am on this stand for the wrong reason."

Counsel's pencil snapped. Maybe, just maybe Coach had changed—

"I should be sitting here to plead for justice, for *fair* play," Coach continued. "Instead I'm asking for *fine* play." He looked me over with ruthless brown eyes. "It's true, Hagen wouldn't make dunk shots. She'd often be outjumped under the boards. But not always. Position is important, as well as height. And position can be learned. Any player could learn rebounding from this." He held up his notebook. Big gold letters said GENERALS PLAYBOOK: PROPERTY OF LEE JR.-SR. HIGH.

Not one General had left court with the crowd. Randy was keeping them together so they could hoist Counsel on their shoulders. I'd overheard their plan for a celebration. They wouldn't have long to wait.

Coach slapped his book and told the judge about basketball. He opened to a page that showed his out-of-bounds play. He held up a drawing of his freeze pattern. "These involve complicated movements on court. Cunningham was right about Hagen. She learns. She learned these in no time. There's a lot more to basketball than simply scoring."

"What?" Rinehart's third question.

"It doesn't matter what. I'm not here to lecture on basketball. I'm testifying about Hagen. *I want her for my team.*"

A groan went up from the Generals. Shrieks from Ruby Jean. Counsel clutched his head. In the middle of this confusion, Rinehart asked his favorite question: *"Why?"*

"Why do the Generals need Hagen?" Coach began a long answer. "Because she plays like a boy. No. No, because she plays well. She has quick moves, fast hands, good vision. She's a scrambler who'll never say ho-hum about loose balls. She'll dive for them anywhere they squirt. She'll be an octopus of a guard. She'll burn many of our opponents when they try to move around her or even through her. Sure, she'll get her share of knocks like the rest of my boys—players. She'll also get *ooooh*'s from the fans because of her technical skill. And her precision shooting. Oh,

Hagen can shoot, all right. The fans will love her percentages. I seriously doubt if attendance will fall off. On the contrary, Arlington takes to a winner. And Hagen's a winner, make no mistake."

Rinehart didn't say *why* or *when* or *how.* Coach kept speaking anyway.

"On offense she'll be a hustling playmaker. She has extraordinary desire. She sets no dimensions for her game. She'll try to learn any move. Think of what she's overcome to get here!"

Think? Rinehart must have dreamed instead, because he didn't ask Coach another question. The witness was forced to ask himself about the locker-room problems. "Showers? We'll figure out something! Uniforms? We'll change at home! Mustaches for the *Herald* Tournament? We'll work everything out as a team! Five heads are better than one."

"Coach went and ruined us," Eugene said loud enough for the front rows to hear.

Randy told his teammates, "She'll have to dynamite the ball from me." Coach gave his famous O'Hara glare until Generals left off grumbling so loud.

Rinehart snapped out of his trance after that. He turned his witness over for cross-examination. Counsel hammered at Coach almost until dinner, but he never changed a word of testimony. Coach sat calm as a guy ahead by a hundred points. When Counsel finally dismissed him, Coach stopped at our table long enough to hand me the playbook. He said, "If Arthur should win your case, I want you to memorize this. Every page. If he loses, don't bellyache."

"What position should Zan learn?" Rinehart had the wits to ask.

Coach O'Hara knew already. "Guard," he said and went away.

Counsel held his temper a little longer. Through clenched teeth he began his summation, but by the time he'd listed every reason I shouldn't be a General, he was blithering: "Not right for a female. Not right! Female. That is all there is to it." He'd given up on logic and his phony kindness.

Rinehart hadn't given up on justice. He wasn't content to win only because Coach O'Hara plugged for a better team. I could tell from my lawyer's summation that he wanted Judge Swain to decide on the principle of the whole case.

"Your Honor, ladies and gentlemen in court, worthy Counsel. For the past two days you people have accused my client of a horrendous offense—being a girl. So she is! She admits her crime."

While this admission sank in, Rinehart strolled back to our Gatorade canteen. He sipped slowly.

"She is a girl. But, as you have heard, she's one who can catch, throw, run, learn plays, and fight for herself. Yet suppose she were not a Zanbanger. She should still be given the chance to become a General." Rinehart crushed a paper cup, his one strongman trick. He was coming to the point. "Judge Swain. For the first time in Virginia, a judge is being asked to rule on this important question: 'Should girls be allowed to play on boys' teams?' I am here today to urge you to say yes. Not only for Zan Hagen but for all these girls."

With a sweeping gesture to the front rows, Rinehart included every ette in his case.

"I ask you, Judge, to grant Lee girls the right to try out for the boys' basketball team. If they fail to become Generals, they fail because they lack speed or shots or moves: athletic skill. For a change, they won't be discriminated against just because they are girls."

Teeny and Joan smiled up at Rinehart, but the others weren't so sure. Bumpy whispered to Aileen, "I could never catch a pass from Fritz." Ruby Jean summed up the twirlers' position. "Boo. Pass it on."

Rinehart paid no attention to the whispers. He eyed the judge to measure his reaction so far. The only clue I noticed was Judge Swain stealing looks at the clock. Rinehart skipped to his final page and read while he pointed.

"Your Honor, if these were your *own* daughters, would you wish them to be second-class citizens? Would you make them stand in front of stoves eternally in order to buy their uniforms? Would you let them walk around injured because they have no team doctor who cares about them? Sir, if these daughters were your sons, wouldn't you want them to receive the best coaching available in Lee High?"

Judge Swain raised his eyebrows but definitely didn't say yes.

"Then why deny your daughters their rights, sir? Do justice to these girls. I will not ask you to treat them like boys. I ask you to treat girls and boys as equal citizens of Arlington County. They both deserve the right to be Generals as long as they have sufficient athletic ability. Thank you."

Cheers broke out in the balcony. E.J. led my mother and Ronald Mergler, Jr., in "Give me an R." Rinehart kept his hand tight against his side in case he felt like waving. He wasn't supposed to before the judge left court to make his decision.

"He won't be out long. He's hungry," Rinehart figured while we waited five minutes, ten minutes, twenty minutes, until the big doors behind the bar swung open again.

"Oyez. All rise."

Judge Swain took his seat, looking at me sternly. He started to read from a note he must have written in his chambers. If he said yes, I'd play basketball this season and Rinehart could finish his science project. If he said no, I'd have plenty of time for study hall. I listened, but all I heard was "Amended: *Regulations Regarding Varsity Athletics at Robert E. Lee High School.*" After that, Randy Boyle was shouting so loud I couldn't hear anything.

Chapter 12

ZANBANGER WINS RIGHT TO WEAR BLUE AND GRAY

Lee Coed Now Riding Generals' Bench After Tryout Ordered by County Judge

BY RONALD MERGLER, JR.

Special to the *Herald*
ARLINGTON, Virginia, Jan. 20—The first girl enshrined in basketball's Hall of Fame may one day be Suzanne (Zanbanger) Hagen, a blue-eyed, towheaded blonde who last night made local history *twice.* Following Judge Titus Swain's dramatic decision in her favor to change school regulations regarding athletics (his amendment reads in part: "No person shall be disqualified from public and high-school teams by reason of that person's sex"), Miss Hagen's lawyer, schoolboy Arthur Rinehart, asked that she be given an immediate tryout for the boys' basketball team. Before court adjourned in raucous disorder, Swain announced trials would be held "at once, after supper." He directed Coach Michael O'Hara to "throw open the doors of the Gen-

erals' gym to every daughter of Robert E. Lee."

Neither of Swain's decisions proved popular. Lee's principal, F. Parnell Manfred (see photograph, page 34), branded the revised regulations "abominable" but gave no reason. A doctor (who asked that his name be withheld) declared the tryouts will have "grave consequences." The school counsel revealed plans to appeal to a higher court in order to "preserve the female race." A group of unidentified boys left Swain's courtroom shouting threats, and perhaps because of all of this, only thirteen girls appeared at the 7:00 P.M. basketball tryout.

For several hours, Coach O'Hara matched these girls against two of his varsity players, Monk Cunningham and Ben Brown. When the dust cleared, only Miss Hagen and her friend, Eleanor (E.J.) Johnston, were still hustling. O'Hara quickly assigned Miss Hagen to be a substitute on his team. He expressed regrets that he has no room at present for Miss Johnston.

Interviewed after the tryout, Cunningham said his testimony has been vindicated. "I swore on Wednesday in court that Zan is good. Now I've seen her shoot, I swear she's even better. She's got a thousand different lay-ups. Her set shots from backcourt are fantastically accurate. Her old-fashioned, underhand free throw looks awkward, but don't let it fool you. It mostly drops in for a point—same as Randy Boyle's one-handed push." Ben Brown agreed, adding, "Eleanor isn't such a shabby lady either. She's pretty and super tall. She never lets up running or pampers herself the way our guy Matello does." (Ed. note: Photographers were barred from this session.)

The basketball season so far has been a disappointment for Lee fans. Generals have played as individuals, not as a team. Consecutive drubbings by Alexandria and St. Vincent's Prep plunged the Generals into eighth place in their Northern Virginia League. Behind at the half last Saturday night against Swanson, Coach O'Hara emptied his bench in an effort to find a winning combination before the Admirals trounced their cross-county rivals. Final minutes of that game were marred by a fistfight between teammates: Eugene Matello and Walter Cadden swapped punches when Cadden replaced Matello in the lineup.

Fifteen games remain in the Generals' difficult schedule. Tonight and tomorrow night they take to the road in action with the Fairfax Wolfmen and the Ft. Belvoir Warriors.

Reached at home by telephone early today, Coach O'Hara indicated he has no unusual plans for his substitute General. "Just say we won't coddle Hagen. We hope to take advantage of her persistence and bravery. She would go over Niagara Falls in a barrel to win." The Warriors were more specific about their probable tactics. George George warned that a defensive play—the stomp—was added to their book within hours of hearing O'Hara's decision to continue the season with a girl on his squad. In Fairfax, a spokesman for the Wolfs would not deny a widespread rumor that the team plans to wear skirts for tonight's contest.

Miss Hagen may well be wearing a barrel in her opener. At Lee High, two lockers containing extra uniforms were broken into sometime last night. All jerseys and shorts disappeared. Principal Manfred predicted further problems for Lee's "integrated team."

The *Herald* agrees. Games will not be easy for their new kid on the block—Zan Hagen. Starting with tonight's 8:00 tipoff, she must face the realities of basketball on boys' turf.

Chapter 13

In school Friday, I stayed out of the turmoil. I was busy being a General. All morning I studied my playbook. At noon I took a hundred set shots, a hundred free throws. Naturally the gym was empty. Naturally the boys were starring in their dispep rally, only it didn't sound so peppy from a distance. The band played off key. Cheerleaders seemed to be weeping. Manfred shouted "Objection, objection" while the chorus sang "Lee High Won't Shine Tonight." Once in a while I heard the plunk of a fallen baton.

E.J. caught my rebounds and snapped the ball back fast, pretending to be Randy, my new mate. Her passes made my fingers sting, but I wanted to practice. Zip. "Ouch." Zip. "Ouch." Zip. "E.J., if only you were playing tonight," I told her on the way to fourth period.

"Wait till next year," Rinehart promised. "Hmmmm—unless a General gets injured this season." He handed me a written test on the playbook. "Do this during math or history, and I'll correct your answers in study hall," he said.

There weren't any true-or-false questions, either. He'd left plenty of blanks to fill. "What are the laws of getting free to shoot?" he'd asked first. I wrote

1. Run faster than your guard.
2. Or fake your guard out of position and go around or over him.
3. Or move behind a teammate and use him to screen your guard.

I underlined important verbs the way I'd learned in English. Then Rinehart had asked, "What are the laws of guarding players like Joe Donn Joiner?"

Joe Donn Who? I almost scribbled, remembering how the Redskins' captain faded in court. But I knew Joe Donn would get revenge on me in a Richmond game, so I put

Guarding High Scorers
1. Press them. That means guard them as closely as possible even if they don't have the ball.
2. Sag on them. That means gang up on them when they are near the basket. Teammates must help each other.

Before the bell rang, I had finished "What are the laws of shooting baskets?" Rinehart gave me an A+ my first this semester. Going home, we jogged slower than usual so I could rest my legs for the Wolfmen.

I rode the team bus to Fairfax. I sat in back with the ball bags. Coach O'Hara used the whole trip for instructions, because thanks to me, we wouldn't be assigned a visitors' locker room, not even at half time. We'd had to change into our uniforms at home. Under my raincoat I wore a plain gray T-shirt and Rinehart's blue gym shorts, brand new. He'd been forging himself out of PE class for years.

I didn't have a number on my "uniform." Who needed it? Every Wolf fan recognized me with catcalls and pennies during pregame shooting. The floor seemed like basket-to-basket copper. Ben and Monk collected fistfuls, saying, "We'll throw these back at the half." DumDum yelled, "Girl, here's a dime looks like." He stuck it in his shoe.

The crowd settled down to watch their Wolfs winning and me benching. I'd been given the very end seat—my spot. Next to me sat Dr. Ableson, hands folded on his little black bag. Between him and Coach O'Hara were our four subs. DumDum went in for Eugene once. When he came out again, he wrapped his head in his warm-up jacket, maybe hoping the score would disappear. Our guys had fallen fifteen points behind already.

By half time the scoreboard read Fairfax 44, Visitors 34. Monk came off court almost crying. Eugene looked ready to kill. Coach made the starters crouch in a circle around him. Quietly he reviewed their mistakes until Randy blurted, "That girl's our mistake. Now we don't even get a locker room."

Coach rocked back on his heels. "Boyle, our team doesn't need a place to hide. But maybe you do. Would you like to go out to the bus? For the season? Or any of you? Now buckle down and help each other. We're a squad, including Hagen." He motioned to me. "You substitute for Matello starting the second half. He's tired already tonight."

Eugene didn't get the chance to slug me. A buzzer sounded. The referee called both teams to the center circle. I reported to the scorer: "Hagen, no number, going in for Matello, number four." I had to shout over the crowd. I had to dodge nickels, even quarters. I had to beware the Wolfmen around me suddenly blitzing off the court. Their coach was screaming "We won't play against a girl!" I had to duck his finger in my face. "I'm taking my *boys* out of this game," he barked. "You're a disgrace to our league."

"You haven't seen me play yet," I said, his finger nearly between my teeth.

"Fairfax forfeits," cried the ref. "Lee wins, two points to nothing."

Monk grabbed my hand and pulled me cross-court. We ran past the bleachers. Big Ben yelled, "Clear the way for a lady." We three Generals escaped to the bus. We climbed aboard with a winning streak of one.

"You were Mr. Cool to their coach," Monk said.

"You beat him man to man," Ben agreed.

But despite our win, the trip home wasn't jolly. The only sound in that bus was pennies dropping from sleeves and DumDum's socks. Monk tried to take up a collection to buy me a real uniform, but no one gave except Ben. He said, "This half dollar almost broke my nose. It should buy you a number at least."

"Number zero," warned Randy from the front.

So Saturday morning I sewed a 0 to my shirt, right below the shoulder blades. Then I shot fouls in the rain. I ran fast breaks up and down the slushy YMCA court. I ran half-speed to Rinehart's lab for lunch over his Bunsen burner. The rest of that afternoon I studied defensive patterns to discover how I could guard the Green Machine, George George, just in case! I caught the team bus after my pregame dinner.

First thing I noticed about the Ft. Belvoir Warriors was their feet. Each player wore one white shoe and one black. "Black for mourning your loss tonight," threatened George from their sideline huddle. Warriorettes paraded the stands with a banner: HAGEN GO HOME.

"Don't let them psych you out," Monk said. Ben slapped my number before he ran out to begin our funeral.

George George nabbed Ben's tip, and the Warriors were off and scoring in their mismatched shoes. George controlled the ball, directing traffic, dribbling, passing, cutting, taking a pass, and scoring on little jumpers from the right side—four times in a row. "That must be the Machine's spot," I whispered to DumDum. "If you go in for Matello, don't let the Machine run to his right."

"Huh? Oh. You."

"DumDum, face him. Get your body between him and the basket. Stand your ground. Don't look in his eyes because he'll give you an eye fake. Watch his chest to see where he's moving. Move in the same direction and he'll bump you. Bump him left. Let him go left. He doesn't like to shoot from there."

"Left?" DumDum shook his left hand. "I dunno."

"Teammate, do it," I said as George scored again. Same spot. Same jumper. Coach called time out with the Warriors ahead, 30–20. At the half, George had made it 34–23.

"Maybe they'll forfeit," Monk hoped in the huddle. Coach didn't let me substitute to find out. Instead he benched Eugene and told DumDum to play the Machine tight. "Force him to his weak side," Coach advised.

DumDum said, "His left!"

Coach seemed so surprised he didn't answer DumDum. "Generals," he said, "help Cadden keep the Machine out of his best shooting range."

"Coach, howsabout I bump him?" DumDum asked.

"Fine, Cadden." Coach sent his players on court without his usual glower.

DumDum bumped him. For the next twelve minutes DumDum collected five fouls, bumping George down the left side. George swished free throws like the perfect robot he was, but for only five points, not his usual ten. DumDum fouled out of the game, smiling. "You ain't so bad looking," he said when we changed places. I was going in for the last few minutes. Score: Fairfax 50, Visitors 45.

A loudspeaker crackled "Number zero, Hagen in the game." The crowd repeated "Zero, zero, zero." I couldn't hear my pals E.J. or Rinehart shout anything.

Monk held the ball, waiting for Warriors to stomp off the court. They stomped, for sure. Every black shoe came down together in some kind of signal. "Do the stomp, stomp," cheered Warriorettes prowling their sidelines. Monk held the ball tighter, wondering what was about to happen. He passed to me and found out.

Every Warrior converged on me. Snorting, blinking, tossing their heads, waggling their hands, they approached in a herd like elephants. They stomped around me, but no one tried to snatch the ball. No one shoved or socked me. All they did was make goofy noises, hold their noses, and wink at me. One called, "Hey, girlie, throw me the ball. I'll throw it right back. Honest."

For twenty seconds I stood in that clump of green uniforms, until I saw a patch of light between two knees. I cocked my wrists. I aimed the ball for the light. I ripped it down past the Green Machine. Then I couldn't see what happened. I could only hear the loudspeaker: "Cunningham scores for the blue and gray."

"So much for stomping," Monk said when we took time out right after his points. "They tried to embarrass you and didn't."

"Shouldn't be rude to a lady. I'll get 'em for that," Ben declared.

Ben got them by scoring. He went on a binge. He hooked from close range. He leaped and stuffed for two . . . for two. He was the tallest guy on the floor, and he began to use every inch. He'd shoot, miss, follow up, tap in for two, run to the other end, block a shot, grab the ball, bring it up court, drive for the basket, slamdunk and say "Stomp you!" The rest of us Generals seemed to trail in his wake on offense. On defense, Monk and I double-teamed the Machine, holding him scoreless for three full minutes. The final shot was sent aloft by Ben. It broke the tie: Generals 61, Warriors 60.

So much for the Warriors. I'd played in my first game. I'd scored the same number as on my uniform:

0

Chapter 14

Journal Entry #1

Rinehart convinced me yesterday to keep track of our basketball season in an orderly, scientific way. He bought me this gray ledger with money he made selling his law brief to Mr. Mergler for a feature on Mr. Manfred's appeal of my case. The *Herald* is also running weekly standings of our Northern Virginia League. I'm gluing the list here.

NVL STANDINGS AFTER FIVE GAMES

POSITION	WON	LOST
1. Claude Swanson Admirals	5	0
2. St. Vincent's Prep	4	1
3. Alexandria Eagles	3	2
4. Ft. Belvoir Warriors	3	2
5. Quantico Lutheran	3	2
6. Robert E. Lee Generals	2	3
7. Friends Academy	2	3
8. Fairfax Wolfmen	2	3
9. John Marshall Judges	1	4
10. Winchester Country Day School	0	5

I'm supposed to write down what I learn every day in practice. Plus the scores of our thirteen more games. Plus my points, if I ever score. Oh, and about how our worst enemies are doing—like the Admirals. They're leading our league. We must beat them and finish number one in order to make the *Herald* Tournament.

Journal Entry #2

Coach O'Hara always spends half of Monday's practice showing films of weekend games. Today we sat together in the darkened boys' locker room. The guys didn't notice me scrunched next to the trophy case. Coach called our errors. "You're not playing like a family," he summed up, starting the second reel. "And your defensive rebounding has never been worse. Only Ben has improved. Look. That's the key play Saturday night." Coach stopped the projector right where Ben took one away from George George. Coach lectured while he pointed to details on screen. He said if we grab defensive rebounds we'll win, because that means we won't be letting the other team shoot two or three times until they score. When we went out on court, Coach drilled us for an hour on positioning. I learned the most important detail about rebounding is to stay between the guy I'm guarding and the basket. I must stand in his path. Not to budge! That's called "boxing out." The player closest to the basket usually gets the rebound even if the guy further away is taller. I learned to snatch the rebound with both hands, bring it to my chest, and stick my elbows out so enemies can't reach and steal the ball.

Journal Entry #3

Rinehart borrowed the films and reran them in his lab. He saw that Randy and Fritz never passed to me once in my three minutes against the Warriors last Saturday night. I hadn't had time to notice in the game, but I've been noticing this week during practice. They play keep-away.

Journal Entry #4

Generalettes lost to Judgettes, but E.J. scored 24 points. Hurray! She's a better shot than Eugene and just as tall.

Journal Entry #5

Another forfeit to us. This time by Winchester Country Day School. Soon as I came out on court late in the game, their players scrammed. I'd worn my new official uniform. Was Winchester frightened by my name, HAGEN, in silk block letters? Or by my number 0? Monk said we should have expected quitters on a team so snooty it won't give itself a nickname.

Journal Entry #6

We barely beat the John Marshall Judges, 57–55. Randy and Fritz scored most of our points. Jumbo Williams substituted, not me. I learned our best plays from the bench, plus I had time to check the bleachers. Judge Swain sat with Rinehart in the second row. Guess His Honor attended because we were playing the Judges.

Journal Entry #7

Coach arranged each practice this week to improve our teamwork. With a Magic Marker, he wrote BE UNSELFISH on our scrimmage ball. He taped the words BLEND TOGETHER to the backboard. Every time the five starters lost the ball to us subs, Coach held up his hand. "Five fingers," he said. "The team that works together like five fingers on the same hand will win the league championship." He told Fritz to pass to someone besides Randy. He tried to make Randy pass off instead of always shooting when he got the ball. "Randy would sooner give blood than give the ball away," Monk says. Coach cracked down on Eugene for not running hard enough. "Keep moving," he said even when Eugene gasped so loud Rinehart heard him from his top-row bleacher seat. Keep moving, look for the good shot, and hit the open man—Coach O'Hara's simple theories of team play. Rinehart calls them laws.

Journal Entry #8

During half time last night against Friends Academy, we heard the goofiest pep talk ever. Here's what happened. Coach decided that at home games we'd use our boys' locker room instead of the sideline bench for instructions. We went in there losing to Friends, 30–24. Coach listed our weaknesses on the blackboard. He reminded Eugene to stop loafing. Coach didn't nag him, but Eugene got furious anyway. He jumped up from his dressing stool and warned the team that I'm a jinx and shouldn't be in their locker room, that I'd cause everyone on the team to play "like girls." Eugene stayed angry next to me on the bench. Monk claims Eugene's whole trouble is he hates to be taken out of games for a sub, especially for me. But he gets too tired running all 32 minutes.

P.S. We won from Friends, 57–53. We lost Saturday's game. I played the last minutes after we were far behind. The Eagles called me "Z-ro" but left me alone. I nabbed one rebound and made three assists. I scored my number, as usual.

Journal Entry #9

Generalettes 34,   Eaglettes 29

E.J. went 12 for 12 at the foul line. We watched the game while we waited to get on court for practice. Coach suggested I tell E.J. not to cross her feet when she's on defense. She should slide them so she doesn't get tangled up when the girl she's guarding changes direction.

Journal Entry # 10

All week we've added tons of new plays to our playbook for Friday's game with Quantico Lutheran. Coach wants to surprise them. He says their assistant coach has been scouting our first nine games, so the Luths know our plays as well as we do. Coach wishes he could scout, but since every team in the Northern Virginia League plays weekend games, he's too busy coaching us.

Journal Entry # 11

Where was Rinehart tonight when we "Z-roed" in on Quantico Lutheran? He missed my <u>first point of this season</u>; a foul shot after I'd been crunched by either a Lutheran or Eugene Matello, I couldn't see who. My swisher raised the score:

Generals 68, Luths 64

with seconds left. Rinehart also blew the chance to examine a basketball injury. Jumbo Williams jumped for a tip-in, came down flat on his back. Dr. Ableson flew off the bench to work his magic, and pretty soon Jumbo was bawling.

Journal Entry #12

We played our annual mid-season breather with the men's faculty last night. We four subs saw a lot of action because Coach wanted to rest his regulars for our rematch with St. Vincent's next Saturday. Our fifth sub, Jumbo, is out for good with a "separated shoulder." I don't know what that means, and Rinehart hasn't been around to explain. He would have loved watching Mr. Manfred, the faculty captain, get smeared by DumDum. My science teacher fouled out when he whirled me around to ask for my three weeks of missing homework. I've been busy being a General. Oh, I sunk that free throw and five others. Teachers foul a lot.

Journal Entry #13

Before Tuesday's practice, we had our team picture taken for the yearbook. Next to me, middle of the back row, stood E.J.! Hurray for our new sub, but not hurray that Jumbo's home in bed.

Journal Entry #14

No time to write this week. Scrimmages brutal. Randy blocks my shots and laughs. Fritz treads my Keds. Eugene whips passes hard enough to break E.J.'s fingers. He fakes E.J. into a corner and says "One girl was bad—but two!" Zap. The ball in her nose. If only E.J. hangs tough! She's not exactly an E.Jbanger. Where is our own personal coach, Arthur Rinehart? He left this list of names in my locker:

Ferdinand Rafferty—He's 6 feet, 2 inches, but a baby. Tell Ben to psych him out.
M.V. Patton—Lousy ball handler. Dribbles too high. Bloops passes. You can steal the ball from him.
Dixie Rowe—His favorite spot is both corners. Force him out of them.

Journal Entry #15

"Actually, Zan, basketball is very scientific." That's what Scout Rinehart told me this morning when I finally found him in his lab. During the past week, he's scouted every team in our league except the Eagles who we wouldn't play again. He's been sneaking into their practices and going to their games so he could prepare reports for us Generals. Scouting reports are like book reports. They explain if the team is any good or not. Also which players have what weaknesses. I'm supposed to memorize everything and tell my teammates so they'll be prepared. Tonight we play St. Vincent's. I'll be guarding M.V. Patton if I get in. I phoned Ben about Rafferty and Monk about Dixie Rowe. Monk donated me the top shelf of his locker in the boys' locker room so I can store extra shoelaces and socks.

Journal Entry #16

I forgot to give the score of our second game with Winchester Country Day School: Us 2, Them 0. Guess who forfeited when they saw me and E.J. both suited up on the bench?

St. Vincent's didn't forfeit. They didn't beat us, either. Ben Brown was the game's top scorer with 24 points, his season high. He held Rafferty to 12 points. Over and over, Dixie tried fakes on Monk, but my new lockermate never let Dixie down the line. Monk made Dixie throw hurried passes and shoot wild shots from too far out. When I went in, the game was already won. Still I stole the ball twice from M.V. Patton. Second time he swore he'd put me in the emergency ward.

Tonight's Saturday, February 18th, exactly three weeks from our final game with the Admirals.

Journal Entry #17

After scrimmage today, Coach O'Hara made Eugene take extra suicide laps. "The harder you sprint here, the easier it will be to keep running in games," Coach advised. Eugene seemed ready to tear off his uniform until E.J. started circling the gym. "Great fun," she called. "Come on." Eugene fell in behind her, muttering, "No girl can outrun me." They raced 50 laps—2½ miles. I waited for E.J. in the steam bath. Coach lets us use it when the other Generals go home. Ben donated a hook in his locker for our towels. He gave us each the combination of his lock.

Journal Entry #18

"Be a family." Coach's theme all four workouts this week.

Journal Entry #19

Monk, Ben, DumDum, E.J., and I met in Rinehart's lab after school. Generals never practice on game days, so we had time to study Rinehart's scouting reports together. E.J. phoned Eugene to suggest moves he could use against Friends Academy. Rinehart baked our pregame dinner in an oven he bought for sterilizing dissecting knives. He explained why the Wolfmen aren't going to forfeit again if I play. Ronald Mergler, Jr., told him it's because the Wolfs have lost every game but two this season, and their coach will be fired if he throws us a freebie.

Journal Entry #20

Generals 68, Friends Academy 56
Generals 71, Fairfax Wolfmen 60

My two-game statistics:

Field Goals 0	**Free Throws 9**
Rebounds 3	**Assists 12**

Journal Entry #21

I'm not supposed to write about schoolwork, only about the Generals' season. Just this note: Yesterday in English, we started work on the exclamation point. My favorite punctuation. Yea!

Now Tuesday. Coach drilled us forever on penetrating zone defenses. After that we gathered in the locker room where he reminded us of league standings by printing them on our blackboard.

NVL STANDINGS AFTER FOURTEEN GAMES

POSITION	WON	LOST
1. Claude Swanson Admirals	10	4
2. Robert E. Lee Generals	10	4
3. St. Vincent's Prep	9	5
4. Alexandria Eagles	8	6
5. Ft. Belvoir Warriors	8	6
6. Quantico Lutheran	8	6
7. John Marshall Judges	8	6
8. Friends Academy	7	7
9. Fairfax Wolfmen	2	12
10. Winchester Country Day School	0	14

Coach underlined our wins with red chalk. He said, "We've been successful while the Admirals have been losing lately. But they are still the team to beat. And look how the others are bunched." He circled six teams below us. "Any one of these could overtake us if we hit a losing streak."

Coach was giving the first formal speech I'd heard him make since in court. I remember this much more: "Team, we have four league games left. We must win our next three, because you can be sure the Admirals will be winning theirs. Then we must beat the Admirals in our final game if we want to be selected for the *Herald* Tournament." Coach passed out scouting reports for our next weekend games. I recognized Rinehart's handwriting on the mimeographed sheets.

By the time we had read the reports aloud together, some guys were getting undressed and heading for showers.

Journal Entry #22

Legs, just get me through one more practice this week. I'll never ask you for another step!

Journal Entry #23

Coach came up to me before the Quantico game. He said, "How are you feeling?" I said, "Fine." He said, "That's good, because you're starting. I promised you'd start if you outscored Matello in scrimmage, and you did." He showed me his line-up card just as he turned it over to the scorer. This is how he listed me:

Hagen, Zan, guard, #0

I expected Eugene to murder me in the team huddle, but he didn't bark or shove. At tip-off, when I shook hands with the Luth I'd be guarding, Eugene called "Good luck" from the bench, next to E.J. Coach O'Hara held up five fingers, the referee tossed the ball between Ben and an almost-as-tall enemy, and—and—there I was, a starting General.

Us starters were anything but five fingers on the same hand. Only Monk and Ben and I worked well together, bringing the ball downcourt, feeding it to Randy and Fritz. Those guys took all the shots for the first seven minutes. Naturally they wouldn't pass to me. They never had, not even in practice.

Coach finally sent in DumDum for Fritz at the second quarter. Our scoring picked up right away. The four of us were four fingers on the same hand. Randy still hogged the ball, doing all his razzle-dazzle moves for the fans: over-the-shoulder dunks, reverse slams, behind-the-back dribbles, twisting jumps. He also groveled for loose balls because we weren't feeding him. When he noticed our strategy, he passed once to DumDum, twice to Ben, once to Monk who threw me a hummer under the basket. I was the open man. I jumped straight up. I let go the ball soft against the backboard. I scored my first field goal of the season.

Ah.

Eugene played the second half. Rested and swifter than usual, he ended up as second high scorer in a close game: Generals 71, Lutherans 68.

Ah.

Journal Entry #24

When we lost to the Warriors tonight, Monk and Ben cried in front of everyone in the gym. I waited until in the locker room. Dr. Ableson gave me some gauze to blow my nose. Rinehart wouldn't cry because he's a scientist, and scientists don't sniffle even if their team won't be playing in the *Herald* Tournament.

Chapter 15

We had lost.

And why mess around keeping track of our losing season? After that game I went right home to hide my dumb journal way to the back of a sweat-shirt drawer. I dropped into bed telling myself, Wait till next year, over and over so I wouldn't cry more. Wait another season, you Redskins—you Joe Donn Joiner. We'll meet you in some tournament eventually. When I get taller and the Generals get more together. Maybe next year Randy and Fritz will pass to me once a game.

I fell asleep replaying the whole 32 minutes of our Warrior disaster. If only we'd won! If only—

Only Rinehart would phone at 6:00 A.M. on a Sunday morning. So I answered.

"The Admirals also lost last night," he said. "Lost." I could hear a newspaper rattling behind his excited voice. Well, not too excited. Not like if his pet mole had broken out of its cage. Or if his pocket calculator had rusted.

"That means—" I wasn't quite awake.

"That means your team—our team still has a mathematical chance for the *Herald* Tournament. If we win our final two games and the Admirals lose one of theirs." He hung up to scheme.

No one else hung up. All day the telephone rang. Monk called. Ben called. They weren't still crying, either. They were more like enraged. They complained about Fritz and Randy. How greedy they are. How we'll have to convince them to join the family or—there isn't any *or.* We need those guys, rotten or not. Eugene said so when he called. He threatened to beat them both up. He could "kick holes in them that would heal in time for our two games left." I said forget it. We'd talk Fritz around, like lawyers would. Randy—well, Randy he could kick once.

After Sunday dinner, Coach O'Hara phoned. I'm supposed to turn in my knee guards he gave me for the Warriors game. He told me to bring my practice gear and extra uniforms to our game films tomorrow. He didn't explain. I stopped trying to figure out why when Fritz Slappy called just before I couldn't get to sleep. Fritz said, "Don't blame me 'cause we lost. Howdja think I could pass to you or the other girl from my seat next to Arthur? Coach benched me, remember?" I remembered.

And here's what everyone said in person at the game film Monday afternoon.

Ben told Fritz, "It's crummy you don't pass the ball to our ladies."

DumDum agreed. "You're making a wrong mistake. Our Zero can score from most spots. Her floor-shooting average's better than yours. I figured it out."

Monk challenged Fritz with "If our girls are no good, throw them the ball and let them prove it."

Fritz looked over at Randy. Randy was reading, so Fritz had to think on his own. He mumbled some answer like "Okay."

Rinehart spoke up, his first time as manager. He asked Randy, "Do you think a pass is thrown only in football games? You're a jerk, Boyle."

I suppose Rinehart couldn't remember the Latin word for *jerk* right then. Randy wouldn't have heard it anyway. He kept reading.

Eugene stayed out of the quarrel until the projector stopped. Then he blurted, "From where I sat Saturday night, it looked as if Hagen never winds down. She covered the Green Machine like a blanket." He threw me a smile.

"She's got the bruises to prove it," Coach O'Hara said. He held up my knee guards. "Generals—you see these? Hagen isn't wearing them in our final two games. She won't need them because you're going to help her, help each other. We're a family." He pointed at two lockers near the whirlpool bath. "Hagen, Johnston, hang up your gear in those and get out on court for practice."

During suicide running, Fritz rolled me the ball—his first "pass" to me. Later when we were scrimmaging, he bounced a bomb off my shin. Some pass! And another off my chin. Each time he put the ball anywhere near me, the whole team except Randy yelled, "Way to go, Slappy." Once Fritz got started throwing me his best passes, he didn't quit all afternoon. Some of them I shot for points. Some I zipped back to him and yelled, "You shoot, Slappy." Nothing fancy. We scored a lot with everyone's help.

Randy stayed in the bleachers after practice, reading a newspaper clipping. Folding it. Unfolding and rereading it. Later Rinehart cut the same part out of the *Herald* sports page and told me to paste it in my journal. So I am.

Journal Entry #25

WASHINGTON AREA ALL-STAR TEAM
(Selected by Ronald Mergler, Jr.)

	NAME	SCHOOL
F	Randolph Boyle	Robert E. Lee
F	Ian Princely	Western
C	Lewis Vanderkallen	Claude Swanson
G	Joe Donn Joiner	Richmond
G	William Moon	Oxon Hill

Coach of the Year
Al Diddle

Rookie of the Year
Zan Hagen

I won't get time to write in my journal the rest of this week because we're having longer, harder practices for the John Marshall Judges Friday night and for the Admirals Saturday night. We must win twice. The Admirals must lose once. Already the *Herald* published the first four teams that qualified for the tournament: Richmond, McKinley Tech, Western, and Oxon Hill. Four more will be added next week when the other leagues have finished their schedules. We have to be one of them!

Journal Entry #26

The freeze! And not against me for a change. We worked it like magic against the Judges last night after we captured a small lead with minutes to play. Monk passed to Fritz who passed to me, and I passed to Ben to Monk to Fritz. Round and around, gliding smoothly, throwing crisply, keeping the ball from the Judges until they deliberately fouled us to get possession. Of course they picked on me. I swished my foul shots. They let me alone.

Judge Swain caught me in the bus parking lot. He introduced me to an even older guy, Honorable Somebody from the Virginia Court of Appeals. Guess they came to see their favorite Judges team get wiped out by our freeze.

Generals 83, Judges 71

Journal Entry #27

Admirals 74, Warriors 65

We're still tied for first with one game left. Tonight we play the Admirals!!!!

Journal Entry #28

Twelve hours ago our family played the Admirals. Smithereen City, as Randy said in court. Tons of reporters covered the game. I'll write here what they missed in their statistics.

Ben Brown outjumped and outfought Vanderkallen, even if he didn't outscore him. I lost track of how many passes Fritz threw me and E.J., but I counted Randy's one to me—a beaut. He leapt, pumped once—twice in midair, and whipped me the ball around his head. I shot for two. E.J. and Eugene subbed for me and Monk. From the bench I could tell they'd been practicing extra together. Their timing was perfect. They knew each other's moves. E.J. taught Eugene her stamina. He taught her his guts. DumDum outthought all the rest of us when he gave the signal for our smartest play. Or maybe he just wanted to remind us to work together. Anyway he held up five fingers to start us on the full-court press.

About what happened after the game: Mr. Mergler puts it better in his column, which I'll stick here in my journal.

When the battle of this century ended, our new Northern Virginia League champs danced off the court and into their dressing room. Laughing, crying, slapping and hugging each other, dousing themselves and photographers with gallons of celebration 7Up, the happy crew cavorted around the whirlpool, then dropped exhausted to their dressing stools.

Some players stared off into space, shaken by their own accomplishments. Some players talked and talked as if they might never believe that ten individuals could feel so close. Their coach moved briskly from ballplayer to ballplayer, saying, "You are really something, you are. A family." Reporters posed the usual questions until most of the stunned players roused themselves to change from their Superman uniforms to street clothes.

Several towel-clad heroes and heroines stayed behind to reminisce with this reporter about their unusual season. I wanted Robert E. Lee captain, Randy Boyle, to sum up his boys' attitude toward sharing health facilities and locker rooms with their fellow girls, but he replied, "Ask Zan here. She'll tell ya."

"None of us noticed," she said. "We've been too busy winning." And win they did: Generals 89, Admirals 85.

Chapter 16

THE *HERALD* TOURNAMENT MARCH 23, 24, 25

First-round Teams

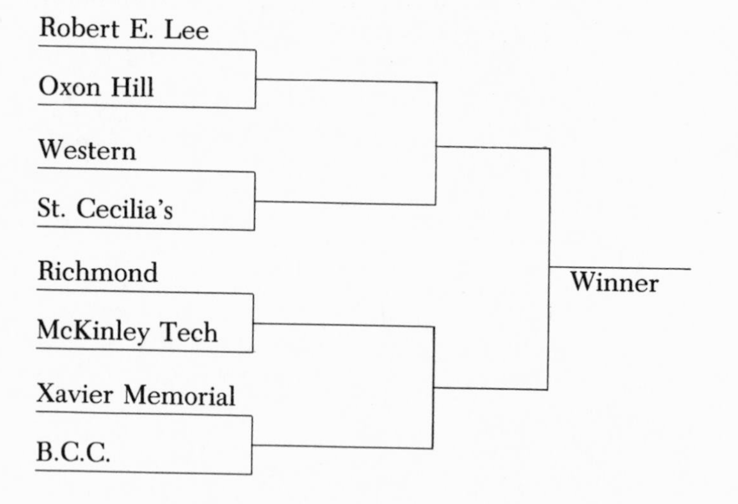

Chapter 17

"Awright, we're gonna grow mustaches for the *Herald* Tournament," Randy announced when the family gathered at Rinehart's lab to study his scouting reports on Oxon Hill.

"Nuts to that," Fritz said. "If Zan and Eleanor can't, it's not fair."

Randy fingered the narrow border of hair along his upper lip. "Okay, howsabout we sew sequins on our shorts or wear perfume?"

E.J. spoke up. "Perfume makes me sneeze. Sneezing might ruin my average."

"And sequins itch," I said.

Coach O'Hara gave us time to joke around and eat our hero sandwiches. Then he said, "We don't need that type of psychological edge. Let Oxon Hill shave their heads for the opener against us. Let the Redskins wear their war paint if they make it to *our* final. They won't beat us on scare tactics. We'll drub them both on basics."

Basics! Back to basics every practice for ten days before the tournament. When he'd toss the ball into play, Coach would say, "Team, if you could just stand and throw at the hoop, you'd score almost every time. You're all good shooters—I know that. But what happens in basketball is that the other team gets in your way. You move, they move. You must take your guard by surprise. Fake him. Today let's see body fakes, head fakes, eye fakes—your absolute best."

Day after day we put out our best until he said, "The game of basketball's made up of a thousand separate plays. Faking. Dribbling. Passing. Jumping, shooting, rebounding, screening, blocking shots, pressing, sagging. You're the best." Coach gave us confidence.

Newspapers gave us zero chance to survive the first round. After all, Oxon Hill stayed undefeated in their Maryland league, didn't they? Their superguard, Willie Moon, broke up games with his Moonshot, didn't he? And our showboat, Randy Boyle, would be trying to win the tournament's Most Valuable Player award. He'd want to shoot, not chase the Moon. Isn't that true?

We knew better.

So did Lee fans. Clusters of them in crepe-paper hats pepped us up at a bonfire rally before our bus left for Washington Coliseum. Ruby Jean Twilly almost burst into flames from her lighted batons. F. Parnell Manfred spoke "a few words for those brave gentlemen who overcame an early-season tragedy in court to attain lasting glory." DumDum made a short reply out the bus window: "What tragedy?" Lurleen Dewey's new cheer was lost in the roar of our motor.

The Lee band and choir bus followed. We heard trumpets when we stopped in traffic. We heard Lee's fight song as we ran out on court for our warm-up. But soon all we could hear was Oxonettes rooting for their bald players, who had captured the lead ten seconds after tip-off.

We weren't afraid of the Oxons' shaved heads. All the same, we played like boobs. We were nervous. A sloppy pass here, a traveling violation there. We ran slow as turtles and stopped in the wrong spots for look-Ma-I'm-throwing-it-up-there off-balance shots. Plus their defense drove us

"Nuts," Fritz kept saying as he wheeled around the basket, looking for an opening. Ben wasn't scoring much. Neither was Randy, with three players sagging on him whenever Randy got to his spots. Monk and I brought the ball downcourt, downcourt, found an open man who couldn't find the basket. In a five-minute stretch, the Oxons reeled off twelve points to our two points.

"Score!" howled the Oxonettes.

"Deeeeeeee-fense!" our fans told us.

"Time out," yelled Randy from his sulk.

Center court to sidelines felt like I was plowing through sand. The shrill Coliseum lights beat down in my eyes. Sweat ran all over my zero. The scoreboard blinked:

LEE 4 OXON HILL 16

Coach's game face met us five in the huddle. "Cunningham, Hagen, you two begin shooting from outside. Sink some thirty-footers. Then their boys can't afford to gang up on Ben and Randy. They'll be forced to guard you."

"Towels," Randy called to the bench. We wiped our hands so we'd stop fumbling.

"That reminds me," Coach said. "Hold your hands

higher. Spread your fingers wider for a pass or to pluck a rebound."

"Water," Randy called for his thirsty team. We drank, licked our wounds, and hurried on court to lick Oxon Hill.

Randy stole the ball to start our spree. He passed to me and I made a swisher from thirty feet out. My guard never left Ben's side. Monk arched one in from thirty-five. His guard stayed draped on Ben. Monk flexed his wrists, rippled his biceps, and sent one in from thirty-six. I took a hope-to-heaven shot from forty. Swish.

Around then the Oxon coach raced the sideline step for step with his players. He screamed, "Guard that Cunningham guy and their number zero girl. Man to man."

An Oxon player moved in on Monk, but I still shot alone. My guard wouldn't come near me. I didn't need my fakes, my pivots, my spins. I could have aimed from a hammock for all my guard cared. Swish. Or slap, kerplop in. My set-shot training was worth every hour I'd stood on those spots. I'd brought us up even by half time.

"Gimme a Z," our bandmaster called. Bam. Bam. Bam went the base drum, following us into the visitors' dressing room. When we reappeared on court, Lee's full chorus sang "For She's a Jolly Good Fellow."

I wish they hadn't, for now Oxon Hill mobbed me whenever I brought the ball over the center line. A tangle of hands tried to snatch it. Even Willie Moon laid off Randy to foul me once. Oxon Hill had fallen for our plan. I passed to unguarded Randy. Slamdunk for two. Monk passed twice to Ben, who hammered four points, two with each hand. By the time those Oxons had figured out our strategy, E.J. subbed for me and started the distance shots all over. Swish from thirty. Swish from thirty-two. Her guard watched her like an audience. He couldn't believe his eyes.

Neither could Lurleen Dewey believe hers. We'd finished the game before she organized a cheer for our hot hands.

> They're our guys
> They're our dream
> Zan and Randy and E.J.
> and Fritz and Monk's high scorer
> Of our team.
> Yea!

"That'll teach 'em not to underestimate the shooting eye of a lady," Ben said on the bus ride back to Arlington. DumDum blew a zero-shaped bubble for our win. Then he asked, "Same scheme for tomorrow night, huh Rinehart?"

"No, not for Western High. Their team runs, runs—a coming-at-you game. There's not a zone defense in their playbook. I've read it." We all asked, "When?" and, "Where?" but Rinehart said, "My secret. I'll have another secret for you on the bus tomorrow night—after we polish off Western."

How could we stop Western, never mind polish?

Here's how. By running with them—faster. By running, scattering, snap passing, firing, rebounding, running, defending the other goal. "Now is when conditioning pays off, team," Coach O'Hara encouraged us at half time. Our strong bench paid off, too. Eugene subbed for me and ran circles around his guard. E.J. raced to her spots. DumDum sprinted for Fritz, for Randy, for Ben. Rested, relaxed with a lead, us five starters took over the last quarter and romped until the buzzer.

LEE 84 WESTERN 74

Lee rooters filled our hair with confetti. Dr. Ableson broke out the alcohol and rubbed our aching hamstring muscles, mine too for a change. That felt good. The bus rocked with our spirit. Our driver beeped his horn in time to "Lee High Will Shine Tomorrow Night."

"We don't need to shine tomorrow night, you guys," Monk shouted over our song. "Richmond will forfeit. Joe Donn Joiner swore so in Arlington court."

Rinehart stood up by the driver. He imitated Joe Donn perfectly. "No man—no way we'd play against females." Rinehart circled his head with a stack of papers. "Team, just in case the Redskins change their minds, I'm giving ycu my scouting report." He handed around the smudgy mimeographed sheets. "Notice what else I've given you," he warned us as we settled back to read in the bright lights of Wilson Boulevard. "I've included *their* scouting report on us!"

As we were going down Glebe Road, Randy asked, "What's all this crazy junk about our team?" He flung the report aside. "Who said I'm a show-off? Who said I'm not such a good captain?"

"And me—I'm not Randy's dupe, whatever a *dupe* is!" Fritz tore up his report.

"Ah, Arthur, am I really this stupid?" DumDum seemed about to blubber.

Ben covered his face with a basketball. "Timid! Timid! Timid!"

Again Rinehart stood up in his lawyerly posture. His glasses jiggled when we crossed the gravelly parking lot. "You're talking about Richmond's scouting report on us. Of course you're all hurt by it. Of course you're angry. But notice the date their scout saw us in action. Early March. Before we'd really changed—before we started to jell as a team. We've overcome our main weaknesses. We're not the same *Homo sapiens.* We'll catch them off guard with our new style."

Coach kept us on the bus long enough to ask, "Arthur, how did you get hold of their scouting report on us?"

Rinehart wouldn't answer that one. Instead he fingered his toad knife and spoke again "in the interest of science." He said, "Study both reports all day tomorrow. Learn their game plan. Learn about the boy you'll be guarding. His errors. His strengths. But most of all, learn about yourselves. Let's know ourselves. And then let's be our new selves."

"That's how we'll shine tomorrow night," Monk said with a basketball-sized smile.

Chapter 18

Showdown time.

Washington Coliseum filled up to its dome. Little kids sold programs with our team picture on page 5, right under the Keds advertisement. Lee fans waved pennants at their "Cinderella Generals," as Mr. Mergler had named us in his column. I took my warm-up, hoping the magic ball wouldn't turn into a red-white-and-blue pumpkin. I chased my rebounds until, near the sidelines, I collided with Ruby Jean Twilly's somersault.

"Zanbanger, I'm gonna be out there twirling for you tonight," she said from the floorboards and flashed her baton.

I almost told her that I admired every maroon sequin on her halter, but I couldn't because starting lineups were being announced.

"And here come those Cinderella fellas, the Generals," a deep voice boomed on the loudspeaker. I had to dash on court and hold up five fingers. Our psych-out signal. Pretty soon the Redskins would know what five meant! They met us mid-court in their war paint—red streaks on their foreheads, red slashes down their cheeks. We shook hands around, all except me and Joe Donn Joiner. "Richmond's here to crush you," he said when we stood facing each other in the center-jump circle, waiting for the opening toss.

"That beats forfeiting," I answered. I gazed up at his harsh lipstick streaks. I was shorter and scareder, but Coach O'Hara knew I'd rattle all five Redskins if I jumped Joe Donn.

"No way, no man, nohow you'd compete against ladies," Ben said with the ball at its highest arch. Then Ben caught Joe Donn's tip and we were playing the final game of that *Herald* Tournament.

To the family's surprise, Randy went into his Most Valuable Player act. He'd catch a pass from Fritz and jump toward the basket, holding the ball with one hand. While he went up, up, up, he'd hang in air, lower the ball to his chest, raise it over his head, lower it again, raise and slamdunk for two. Pure hotdog! Or he'd fake his man, Laddie Griffen, into a corner, then varoooooom! One long Boyle-step and he'd be past Dwayne all the way to the bucket. Down the middle one-handed, two-handed, backhanded, Randy shot and swished, shot and shouted, "Two big ones . . . two more biggies."

Lots more biggies from Randy's bag of tricks on defense. What a showboat! Blocking balls with smacks that echoed to the dome, jumping into orbit to pin a shot from Joe Donn Joiner against the backboard, Randy came down waving the ball at the drum and bugle corps—not ours but the Redskins'. Wow, what nerve! Their buglers blew sour notes. Redskin cheerleaders jeered. Even our family wanted to give Randy a swift kick.

But wait a minute. Our team learned something. Randy's flashy moves counted same as Monk's modest set shots and Ben's tip-ins and Fritz's fall-away jumpers and my dumb foul shots. Showing off scores points too, you know. We were ahead at the quarter

LEE 20	RICHMOND 16

"You really are something, you are, Boyle. But you're no family man!" Coach O'Hara half kidded our high scorer in the huddle.

"Great shooting." E.J. patted his shoulder.

"You're defending like a pro, Randy," I said and meant it. First time I'd ever told him.

Randy's answer? "Zan, you got a bad cut above your lip. Who belted you?" He wiped my blood on his shirt and called Dr. Ableson for iodine. "Fix her," he said. DumDum whispered he thought Joe Donn had scraped me in a rebound hassle, but I really couldn't remember. After seventeen games this season, I was used to playing with guys' arms in my mouth.

The second quarter began with a whole other Randy. Maybe because he was double-teamed, triple-teamed, maybe because he wanted to cross up the Redskins' scouting report—whatever—he passed to all of us, me and Monk most. I shot two from my favorite corner, two from way outside the foul circle. Monk made a driving stuff and a reverse lay-up. Then, for what seemed like minutes, I stood holding the ball, with Joe Donn's finger nearly stabbing my eyes. "Don't shoot anymore," he commanded.

All the same I shot—a soft jumper that Joe Donn blocked and fouled right back into my face. He yelled, "I'm telling ya, don't shoot. Ever!" Monk dove for the loose ball, by now bounced off my blood-streaming nose and rolling toward the Redskin bench.

Randy Boyle dove for Joe Donn Joiner. They locked arms and crumpled to the boards. Those team captains brawled like desperadoes. They punched ears, punched the foul line, punched their teammates, who quickly gathered to unwrap them. The umpire nearly lost his black-and-white striped shirt leading both boys off court. "Foul on Joiner for bashing number zero. Technical on both these boys for fighting," the ref called to the scoring table. "I'm not allowing these two back in the game until second half."

"Time out," Fritz called, taking right over as captain. I gave Fritz a woozy salute of thanks.

We grouped around Coach O'Hara, who didn't waste breath scolding Randy, just motioned him to sit down, simmer down. DumDum filled Randy's place in the huddle. My nose felt like it was hit by a wrecking ball, but I wanted to play, so I didn't complain. Coach warned us, "Team, this is not a slaughterhouse. Forget what Joiner did to Hagen. You're ahead in points, in pride. No bloodletting necessary."

"Ice bag," shouted Fritz to Dr. Ableson. They swapped turns touching it to my nose. Coach told me to make the foul shot, my best revenge on Joe Donn. Rinehart mourned my bloody nose by holding his own and winking to the Redskins' bench, where Joe Donn was being worked over by a doctor with piles of swabs, tape, and for all we knew, frankincense. Randy Boyle had put a few dents in the Donner for me.

"I feel like it," I said when the buzzer summoned us to the foul line. "I'll shoot."

"Attagirl," Fritz said, lining up the family ready to catch my rebound—in case I missed. Suppose I did have a ninety-percent average. I still could miss if my nose swelled more to block my vision.

The Redskins lined up, too, looking me over with grins. My zero didn't show. It was covered with blood. Totaled, I'll bet they were thinking about me. When the referee handed me the ball, Laddie Griffen hissed, "Miss it."

"You'll pay for that," Ben warned, but by then my point was up on the scoreboard and our cheerleaders were ranged along the sidelines screaming into their megaphones.

Give me a Z
Give me an A
Give me a ZAN
ZANBANGER ZANBANGER
YEA! YEA! YEA!

I only half listened, even when our band's brass section blew a twenty-one-trumpet salute. After the jump ball, which Laddie Griffen tapped to us by mistake, all I concentrated on were shoes slapping the floor as our teams traded baskets. Generals—skid and shoot. Redskins—run, jump, and shoot. Slide through the defense, glide toward the corner, and shoot over Joe Donn's substitute. Drive, spin, control the ball with one hand, fend off defenders with the other—and shoot. Spring for a rebound, wriggle around a hedge of hands, pass, catch, and shoot. Put three fakes on a red shirt and shoot. Dribble through a maze of red war paint and shoot. Shift the ball from right hand to left, stretch, stumble but shoot. Move past their moves. Take an all-or-nothing shot a second before the half-time buzzer.

Buzz.

The family scored its thirteenth field goal of the second quarter.

LEE 50 RICHMOND 47

In the steamy dressing room, we wiped off sweat, planning to work up more. We gulped Gatorade. Coach O'Hara and Dr. Ableson sat on the floor helping us retie our shoelaces and retape our socks so they wouldn't droop. Coach said, "You have sixteen minutes left to play—sixteen more minutes of everything you have to *give to each other.*" His speech was over before we knew he'd begun.

Rinehart's advice lasted longer, naturally. He jumped up on the rubdown table to holler, "*We* have work to do. Stop Rex DeLeo in the pivot. He's not fooling you with his moves. He's frightening you with that war whoop. Ben, pretend you're a tomahawk and crowd him."

Ableson said, "I have discovered tonight that their boy Dwayne Yelverton is playing against his doctor's advice. Something about mononucleosis. He's bound to wear down this half."

"Whose man is Yelverton?" Randy asked.

Fritz said, "Mine." E.J. said, "Mine." Together they said, "Ours." They had been alternating forward.

"Press Yelverton," Randy demanded. "Hard. Harder than you've ever pressed anyone."

DumDum tapped his head with his forefinger. He said, "Our second worst problem is fouls. Fritz, you got four—one more and you're out. Randy, you got three—two more and you're out. We need your tall height."

I told Randy, "We need you, Captain, so don't slug Joe Donn even if he uses my ear for a bank shot. I can take it."

"Our first worst problem is me," DumDum continued. "I only got six points. I'll score this many more." He held out his hands, some fingers up, some down.

We refreshed each other with hugs all around and stormed out for the second half. We felt tension building in that muggy Coliseum. The Redskin side howled "Hit Zan again, harder" to Joe Donn every time he high-stepped toward them with balls spinning on his fingertips, Globetrotter-style. Our side chanted "Fly, Ben, fly" when he leaped to rebound our practice shots. Once when I got close enough, I heard Ben say, "Our pep squad's asking the impossible. Fly? Me?"

Eugene said, "If I can suicide sprint, you can fly."

Randy said, "We'll fly together," and dribbled in time to a drum. He passed to E.J., who was going to start the second half in order to save Fritz's fouls for the fourth quarter. Lurleen watched us working together and organized this cheer:

They're our girls
They're our dream
Randy and E.J.
   and Eugene and Zan
Score for . . .

And suddenly, at the sound of a buzzer and whistle, there E.J. was psyching out Joe Donn in the center-jump circle. She stood almost eye to eye with his black eye. The basketball rose, rose, rose. She called, "Mind your injury, Joiner." Joe Donn lowered his hands and E.J. sprang to tap the ball to Randy, who was back in the game, back in the family. Randy twisted away from two guards. He sped a pass to Ben. Ben flew to stuff two points, starting the wildest quarter in any tournament history.

You never saw such ferocious play! Redskins smothered our guys when we tried to help each other. They picked apart our screens. They clogged the middle. Nicking turned to bumping turned to jostling. Jostling turned to three rebounds in a row because Ben got so angry he persuaded every part of his gangling body to move in the same direction: UP. All us Generals flew up, then up and down the court, our minds racing ahead with plays that Randy called in our game code. Our shooting blew hot and cold. One minute we were radar accurate; the next we made such idiotic shots as the basketball up through the net, not down.

"Doesn't count, doesn't." The ref signaled. Gleeful shouts rattled the dome. Paper cups fell around us like grenades. Seconds later a Redskinette backflipped into Eugene's whirling fake.

Technical foul, signaled the ref. "One shot for Matello."

Randy encouraged Eugene. "Take a deep breath same as Zan does. Bounce and feel the ball same as E.J. You'll make it." We lined up to bursts of "Miss it" from Redskin fans. At the foul line, Eugene heard the usual whistles. He saw the same old shoulder flinches from Laddie. Eugene answered the pressure with a Swish. He made that one point and two more on a steal by Randy from Joe Donn. Randy passed to Eugene cutting across the foul circle. In one energetic motion, Eugene caught, pumped, and lofted a beauty, tying the ballgame, end of third quarter.

LEE 80 RICHMOND 80

That Coliseum was an oven. Underfoot, a black sideline seemed wavy in the heat. A haze of smoke hung over our heads, but still the lights beat down on us in a circle with Coach and Rinehart and our doctor toweling away the third-quarter jitters. "Let's not beat ourselves," Randy warned. Rinehart pointed to two old guys in our cheering section. I recognized Judge Swain. He held one edge of a banner that said "Lee High Loses Appeal of Hagen Case." Monk saw it, too, and asked me if I could play third base, what with baseball season starting tomorrow and all.

"I'm a shortstop. I'll explain after we win," I told my backcourt brother.

Fourth quarter; final game; *Herald* Tournament.

Basket to basket we never let up running. In a minute their Yelverton passed out. In two minutes our Slappy fouled out. Our Ben held Rex in check, but their guy Fran Ross broke loose with a twenty-footer, with two sweeping dunks, and with his masterblast shot over DumDum's leap. Those eight points put them way ahead. Seeing the scoreboard click so far in their favor, we rubbed our eyes in disbelief.

LEE 90	RICHMOND 98

Our final time-out ticked past. We thought we were done for, but anyway we piled our hands up and said "Us five" for the last minutes that basketball season. Joe Donn shouted, "Eat your hearts out," from the Richmond huddle.

"Play your hearts out," Rinehart suggested softly, maybe because he was crying—not exactly the man of science right then. "Hearts," he wept, and pounded his chest around where his heart might be. Up till then I wasn't sure he had one.

We took his advice and ran with it. We whipped the ball downcourt, person to person. Monk to me, me to Randy, Randy to Ben, Ben to—find the open person.

E.J. scored.

We finally knew each other's moves. Shoulders overlapping on the next rebound, fingertips touching the same sweatwet ball, Monk's medal around my neck, Randy's freckles in my eyes, we drove down the sidelines for another basket.

Randy scored.

Our eyes never left each other. Randy's green ones

met E.J.'s with a smile when she stole the ball from Joe Donn and passed to Monk. Monk's blue eyes said "Still a chance, a chance to win," as he mashed his fiercest shot past Joe Donn's puffy eye.

Monk scored.

Fritz, Eugene, and DumDum waved their towels from the bench. Rinehart twirled his rolled-up program. Help came from everywhere at once. Ben, our flyer, out-rebounded Rex. Randy, our leader, signaled the perfect play. Monk, our sophomore, outtoughed two guards. E.J. banged past their nameless substitute. We swarmed down the middle. Red-white-and-blue came alive in our hands. That ball loved us. Floorboards seemed to kiss our feet. The buzzer waited for Ben's winged points.

He scored.

We needed another basket to win. Legs, take me there—take us all there, I said to mine. Randy's look was green light again. His steal filled my hands. No time to dribble. Not to fake anymore. I felt tall—taller than myself. I shot from my spot at the final buzzer. My eyes didn't bother to follow the ball's flight. Instead I watched Coach O'Hara race on court with Rinehart.

Coach lifted me to his shoulders. Rinehart tried to hoist Randy. Around us every teammate raised another. The scoreboard lit our season.

LEE 100 RICHMOND 98

We had won. We had won each other.

Format by Kohar Alexanian
Set in 11 pt Gael
Composed, printed, and bound by The Haddon Craftsmen,
Scranton, Penna.
Harper & Row, Publishers, Inc.